Techno-Myth

Techno-Myth
By Michael A. Rodriguez

BRYSON

PUBLISHING

THE HOME OF INDEPENDENT WRITERS

This edition first published in 2023 by Wandering Minds Publishing located in Fort Washington, Maryland.

www.WanderingMindsPublishing.com

ISBN: 978-1-959665-02-1

Cover by Michael A. Rodriguez

Manufactured in the United States

To those who helped me reach the stars.

Prologue

Owen hated the mornings. Nothing good ever happened during the morning. In his experience, nights were historically much better. Only the elderly and small children ever complained about the night. Aside from scary stories told around the tavern fire, night held many great things: fine food, good friends, seductive women, potent drinks, and when you finish, you could just pass out and lose yourself in the realm of dreams.

Mornings were just the opposite. They demand your work and force you to confront the harsh reality of life. Painful headaches, a consequence of actions taken the night before, frequented mornings. That, or the cold realization that you fell asleep outside.

This morning was no different. He stumbled across the misty, uneven ground in front of him. While on his way that morning to set up a stall in the nearby village for the local bazaar, something agitated his horse, causing it to burst off the side of the road, pulling his loaded cart with it.

He didn't have a clue what spooked his old mare, but there were many things in this corner of the kingdom that would find them both a tasty snack. Another reason for him to hate this particular morning.

Following the blatant destruction of the cart wasn't difficult, but navigating the remains of dead trees and ruts that littered the ground, threatening to break his ankle with every step, was a different story. To make things worse, the rising fog grew stronger the farther he wandered off the path and into the forest.

Cursing his luck, he rounded a tree as a branch swung at his face, leaving a welt across the groove of his eyes. He took a moment to release his frustrations, cussing loudly for whoever could hear him. He blinked his eyes several times, finding that tears and pain blurred his vision. Cautiously stepping forward, he reached out, hoping to steady himself with a nearby tree, only to find a dead branch that gave way as soon as he put his weight on it.

Peering through tear-filled eyes, he noticed a desolate, fog-covered landscape had replaced the forest. He stood on the edge of the Deadwoods.

Taking a quick gulp, he gathered himself and, with a piece of fabric from his shirt, covered his mouth. The Deadwoods hadn't always been like this. Tales regarding this area told of an ancient human weapon attack that forever scarred this land and covered the ground with toxic fog. Despite the desolation, the Deadwoods weren't lifeless. Monsters roamed these lands, always hungry. Only those with a death wish entered the Deadwoods for longer than a few seconds at most. Everyone knew that anything that went in there never came out again.

Deciding on whether to continue his way to town

and pawn off the boxes, or give up and head back to the previous village for a fresh start, a piece of worked wood caught his eye. Peering through the fog, he found a pit in the earth, a sinkhole, that had the barest tip of his wagon sticking out of a dark cavern at its very back. If the wagon was still upright it was possible he could salvage the supply run entirely, if his horse was still alive all the better, either way, this would indeed be a strange tale he could use to get himself a couple of free drinks at the local tavern.

"There I was minding my business when the horse gets spooked and runs off the road into the forest," he practiced as he looked for a way into the sinkhole. "Naturally, I took after it as any good supply runner would and, after a while, tracked it down to the Deadwoods." Sliding down a natural-made ramp on the side of the sinkhole opposite the dark entrance, he tripped a bit and tumbled forward into the bottom of the pit. Groaning a bit, dusted himself off as he tried to recall what he was about to say next.

"Obviously, I'm not a fool. I was about to cut my losses when, out of the corner of my eye, I spot the cart in a pit. So I say to myself, 'no use in leaving empty-handed', and I descend the pit to grab it," he recounted as he approached the cart.

The story was good, but it was missing something. He entered an opening on the other side of the sinkhole. Inside, he saw his wagon, relatively intact. One of the wooden spoked wheels had cracked, but nothing a talented carpenter couldn't fix. Unfortunately, the harness connecting the horse to his wagon had snapped. The horse was gone. Glancing around in the dark tunnel, he dared a quick whistle, trying to call for his horse. It was just blind hope, he knew, but it didn't hurt for him to take it.

Thinking back to his story, he realized what was missing. There was no action in it. The stakes were low. Nothing threatened his chance of survival. What his story needed was a monster or two. As he came to this revelation, he heard a faint whine come from further down the dark passage in front of him. Risking another whistle, he heard a similar response, only this time louder and more distraught. Pulling his knife from its sheath, he began walking down the tunnel. "There were two...no, three of them. They were as big as a horse and just as ugly with long teeth and sharp claws and they made clicking sounds," he said as he saw the outline of an equine figure in the tunnel.

Approaching closer, he saw it was indeed his horse, but it was laying down in the small tunnel as if it had collapsed. "What's the problem girl?" he asked as he kneeled down and ran a hand along the beast's side.

It didn't take him long to find the problem as his hand ran across several deep gashes on the horse's side. In one of them, he found the remains of a piece of wood. He pulled his hand back. He didn't have to look at it to know it was covered in blood.

As he sat there considering whether it was kinder to end the creature's suffering or attempt to save it, he heard a sharp tearing sound as something fell from the ceiling. A strange appendage groaned as it tried to descend.

"Error, intruder. Error, malfunction."

Readying his knife, he pointed it in both hands at the thing. He had never used one in self-defense before. He normally hired mercenaries to accompany him through dangerous areas.

"Error Malfunction. Deploy. Intruder Error."

Something sparkled next to the appendage as he

watched in horror. He dropped his knife and turned toward the entrance at the start of a dead run. *Fuck all this*, he thought. He could get another horse, a new wagon, and do double delivery to make up for the lost cargo. Only fools entered the Deadwoods. He was no fool.

Just as he neared the wagon, a deafening silence followed. Owen never had to worry about mornings ever again.

Chapter 1

"I can't remember a time we didn't have to fight. In the history of humankind, it's the one thing that never changes. Our driving factor, I guess. When times of peace finally catch up with us, it doesn't stay for long. The world is at war once more, and for this, I see only sorrow."

Nora looked up and found her small class of children probing at the gazebo dirt with sticks or gazing out into nowhere. She took the kids out of the classroom that afternoon to learn in one of the city's water gardens. She had hoped a change of environment would help them retain today's lesson. But as she looked over at them, she realized it had the opposite effect. Their attention focused on everything but what she read to them.

Closing her eyes for a second, she let out a soft, disappointed sigh. They seemed to care so little about the Precursors and their remaining teachings. How could they ever expect to be ready for the long-awaited return and accept the gifts they are to bestow upon the world, as the

Followers have foretold?

It probably didn't help that she technically wasn't a teacher, but an artificer substituting to make rent while she tried unraveling the mysteries left behind by the precursors. She hadn't yet made a name for herself, either. Most of her work was unfruitful or disproven by more notable artificers.

Silently, she closed the leather-bound book, having finally finished reading through it. It contained the last writings of an unknown precursor, a relic of the past. Their work was not as well-known as others, but it was her own particular find among the ruins. The words seemed to have a hidden meaning every time she read them, one that nagged at her constantly. As she turned the book over, she felt the worn inscription of a name on the old frayed leather, indiscernible from the rest of the book, but still there if you looked closely.

The tower bells rang eight times, alerting the city of noontime. The children scampered up on their feet at the sound, rushing off to the marketplace or back home. They said their goodbyes to her, but she knew they hurried to be far from the words of the old. Nora stood up and, with a flip of her hand, brushed her long hair behind her ear, out of her face.

"My dear Nora, you look more radiant each day," spoke a cavalier voice behind her.

"And you, Rylan, need bells around your neck," she said, turning around to spot the handsome knight of the King's-Glaive. "Honestly, how are you so silent for a person so tall? And a knight nonetheless."

"I've had lots of practice hiding from beautiful maidens," he joked. "That is…when I'm not on duty."

"Oh, really? What brings a Glaive in search of a scholar such as myself?" she asked in a playful tone. She knew Rylan as a simple man. One who strongly preferred the sword to a history lesson.

"Well, I was going to leave you in suspense, but in all seriousness, this is a pretty important matter," he answered with a sigh.

"What's wrong, Rylan?" she probed. Something was bothering him; he was never one to skip to the important part.

"A week ago, we sent a search party to the Dead-woods," he answered hesitantly. "We tasked them to look for a lost supply runner, and they came across an entrance to a cave. Inside, they found the runner's wagon, hidden and untouched, and his body lying next to it. It appears he burned to death. Upon further inspection, they found that the entire back of the cave had fallen away, revealing a path leading deep underground. They headed down and found an enormous set of steel Precursor doors. Upon receiving their report, the king ordered me to assemble a search and investigation team to continue exploring the ruins. I came here to ask you to join us."

"Of course I would like to go!" she nearly screamed, excitement bubbling in her chest. "Let me just grab a few things."

"Ok, we'll be ready to leave this afternoon. Meet us by the southern gates. Just make sure you are prepared for anything," he said as he walked out of the gazebo and into the gardens.

Nora squealed in excitement. She quickly gathered her long dress in her hands and ran out of the water gardens and toward the west side of the city. The sprint was a short one for her as she darted down back alleys and in between buildings toward her house, but the passing of every second felt crucial as she skirted from one dark alleyway to the next.

When she reached the far side of the city, she barreled through the plaza, straight into the entranceway of her home. Her excitement was near intoxicating; she felt like she had taken hold of a lightning bolt. Overwhelmed, she stripped her house of everything she would need for the trip. The thought of exploring a newly found Precursor ruin was too big of an opportunity to miss. She thanked Rylan under her breath a thousand times as she tossed garments and other items into an old leather carrying pack she had kept from her grandmother.

As she searched the house for her relic kit, she imagined the wonders she might find at this new dig site. Would there be more inscriptions of the elder dialect, or would she find another amazing invention like the power orb? Then, stopping in the middle of the room, she dragged out the notebook of the long-forgotten author she possessed. Would she find more of their work in these ruins, or even a fragment of something else they had owned? Maybe she would find the answers to what the writing was trying to convey. She carefully slipped the book into her pack and then changed into more suitable travel attire.

At about 1:30, Nora was finally ready. Belted trousers and a green tunic replaced her long blue dress. From her belt hung a few odd screwdrivers she made for inspecting old precursor items, a bag of sand, long tough twine, and a magnifying lens. She pulled her hair back into a ponytail, keeping all but a few pesky strands of hair from her face. Looking herself over in the mirror, she felt all the readier for her adventure. What had been a lady in fine clothing was now replaced by the image of an adventurer. Grabbing a cloak off the living room peg, she exited the house and locked it up before heading toward the city's southern gate.

***

A few hours later, she lost sight of the city of Somnium. It was a strange feeling to not see the cities white walls and towers on the horizon anymore.

"Miss the white walls already, lass?" came the jeering response of the man beside her on a horse.

"Not as much as you'll miss your wife, Burnie," she teased back to his scruffy, bearded face.

Burnie was one of the few companions accompanying her and Rylan to investigate the caves. For a man of about 40, he still looked fit and in his prime even his tanned skin seemed to retain its original youth. The only sign of age was a few grey strands that peppered his black hair. His attire resembled a sailor, his demeanor did as well; though he never claim which ship he had sailed on, he spoke of his time on the great ocean. The only truth to this claim hung around his throat. A necklace of Horker and Razorback teeth, which is awarded along the coast to brave sailors. But that wasn't what she found weird about the man at all.

What she couldn't wrap her head around was why he wore an eye patch if he wasn't visually impaired.

"That old teapot?" he asked, with a bout of laughter. "She practically threw me out the door when she heard."

Another bout of laughter followed this as he sped along on the back of his horse.

"I wouldn't worry about him, Nora," the long-coated man on a horse in front of her replied. "Burnie will get along just fine."

His name was Gus, the wizard of the party. He was good friends with Burnie and had both been on quite a few outings together with Rylan before. Aside from his dirty brown coat, Gus was unlike any other wizard she had encountered. First off, unlike other wizards who dressed in the finest silks, Gus wore simple clothes that one might expect from a farmer or a tailor. He also didn't carry the usual pouch of trimmings and ends that were typical of wizards. Gus lacked these things, except for a pair of gloves he wore that had weird circular runes stitched into the fabric.

Aside from these oddities, Gus looked like an average court politician, especially with how he seemed to carry himself.

"Yeah, don't worry about us, lass," Burnie interjected. "Worry about yourself and all the many ways you could die out here in the wild."

"I'm well aware of the wildlings. Thank you very much," she said.

"You think wildings are the only things out here?" asked Gus in disbelief.

"Of course not. I'm not dumb," she replied sarcastically.

"Oh, so you know about the Boggins as well, do you?" asked Gus.

"Ugh, I hate those things with their grotesque and mossy bodies, but they are not half as bad as phantoms," responded Burnie from the front.

"Uh, no kidding. I'd rather face a Boggin than a

bunch of them any day," replied Gus with a visible chill.

"I thought phantoms were just a bedtime story?" she asked with a brief pause.

"Oh no, they're as real as my aunt Petty's neck fat," Gus answered, pulling up ahead next to Burnie. "Shadowy creatures of pure malice and hatred…every one of them."

"You're not wrong," replied Burnie with a quick glance at the tree line on the side of the road. "I've seen one destroy an entire village in an afternoon."

"All right, guys, knock it off," called Rylan from beside Nora. He had been riding behind the group for a while and just caught up with them. "This is Nora's first time outside the walls. Let's try not to scare her away."

"Okay, Rylan. Whatever you say," answered Gus with a backward glance.

"Besides, if I wasn't sure she could protect herself, I wouldn't have brought her along," finished Rylan with a look that challenged the other two to disagree.

"I'm fine with her being here so long as she knows what's out there," responded Burnie.

"I completely understand that, Burnie, but I doubt we'll encounter anything besides a few woodmen," replied Rylan in his most assuring voice, "and they basically keep to themselves so long as they're not disturbed."

"Can't argue against that," answered Gus from his mount. "We shouldn't really encounter anything too dangerous."

They continued on in semi-silence for a while longer, the only perforation being the occasional whistle of a strange bird. It wasn't until Burnie started talking about punching a horse did the conversation begin to really kick off. After a while of this chatter, Nora felt less like a stranger among this band of friends and more like a member herself.

Before long, they stopped underneath a wild grove of flower willows; the sun playing off the clouds in a beautiful color show. Nora took a whiff of the air and noticed the sweet smell of willow blooms.

"Spring blossoms are in bloom," she stated as she searched for a suitable spot to set up.

"Hopefully it doesn't attract any wild animals," muttered Gus as he tied off his horse to a tree, "especially squirrels."

"What's all that about?" Nora asked while staring after Gus.

"Gus had a terrible incident with a squirrel on one of our last adventures," Rylan answered with a huge grin.

"It pissed directly at me!" Gus replied in exaggeration.

"Anyway, let's get a fire going so we don't attract any actual threats," Rylan said with a good chuckle.

"I'll get it started right up," volunteered Burnie with a swagger toward the nearest tree.

"And with that, I'll check the perimeter," Rylan said after tossing his bedroll on the ground. "I'll be back in about ten or twenty minutes. If not, well, Burnie knows what to do."

"Right, tell the women goodbye and burn any risqué documents in your hidey-hole," Burnie answered while ripping at a tree branch. "Got it! Have fun."

As Rylan walked away, Nora rolled out of her bedroll on the ground after kicking away several rocks. It felt weird not having a roof over her head, but it was liberating. Slowly, she laid down to test her bed and looked up at the orange-tinted sky quickly fading to purple and then to starry night.

"Enjoying the twilight?" asked Burnie from somewhere to her left.

Looking over, she noticed him crouching over a plentiful heap of sticks and dead branches, structuring them into a teepee.

"I enjoy watching the sky change color; it's beautiful," she answered.

"After spending time at sea, everything's pleasant weather on a regular day for me. Kind of lost its splendor, in a way," he answered, followed by a slight groan as he pushed himself up from his crouch.

"That should do it."

The teepee he erected looked like a collapsed mess with no direction of construction. The only workable thing Nora could see was the circle of rocks surrounding it.

"Well, are you gonna light it?" she asked sarcastically, noticing the quickly encroaching darkness of night.

"Oh, Gus!" Burnie called out as a wicked grin swept across his face.

"What do you need?" Gus replied angrily from a small tent set up out of the way of the fire.

"Could you please come help with the fire?" requested Burnie while quickly hiding his grin beneath his best poker face.

With a great sigh, Gus dragged himself from his tent and stood to the side of the fire pit opposite Burnie. "What do you need?" Gus asked with a frown across his face. "I thought you said you had the fire under control?"

"I thought so as well, but unfortunately, my tinder box burnt out the last trip. Think you could start the fire with a bit of magic?" Burnie asked with a serious face.

"Burnt out tinder box? When has that ever stopped you from making a fire?" Gus questioned, his voice filling with antagonism.

"Look…just use some magic, dude. It's not a big deal," Burnie replied angrily as he sat down across the fire pit from Gus.

"Ugh, fine, but I still don't see why you need my help," Gus said begrudgingly as he bent down over the logs and conjured a tiny spark of fire in his hands.

As soon as the fire was within sight of Burnie, he quickly took a swig from a bottle of something blueish, then spit it in a fine spray at the open flame in Gus' hands. As soon as the mist touched the fire, an explosion erupted in Gus' face, engulfing the fire pit and lighting the firewood instantly.

Gus rolled on the ground in front of the fire with his hands on his face, shouting as if to summon a deity. Burnie doubled over, laughing at the sight of his friend rolling around. Putting a hand to her mouth, Nora couldn't help but keel over laughing either at the sight of her companion.

"What the fuck?" Gus shouted as he stood up from rolling around, his big bushy eyebrows smoldered. "You sick fuck! Why would you do that?"

"Hahaha, you should have seen your face," Burnie crooned through his laughter.

"Fuck you, man! I'm going back to my tent!" Gus yelled as he stomped off to his tent.

Recovering from her bout of laughter, Nora wiped tears from her eyes. She noticed a happy calm settle over Burnie as he wiped his eyes with one hand and used the other arm for support. He smiled into the distance as the fire cast shadows across his face. At that moment, he looked old to Nora. An aged man who had lived a good life, but still had more living to do.

"Hey kid," he said out of the corner of his mouth.

"Yeah, Burnie?" she asked, sleep weighing heavily on her eyes as she stared at the fire.

"Don't worry about fitting in, okay? Because, in my book, you're always welcome," he said with a slight smile.

"Thanks, Burnie," she said, laying her head down on her crisscrossed arms.

"No problem, kid. Now get some rest. I'll wait for Rylan and take the next watch," he said, taking a swig from the bottle of bluish liquid again.

"Okay, goodnight Burnie." She drifted off to sleep as the flames danced shadows around her.

Chapter 2

The next morning, Nora woke up and ate a makeshift meal of fruit and sausage with Rylan and Burnie. Gus busied himself packing up his tent while they finished their breakfast. After putting the fire out, they mounted their horses and traveled down the dirt road again, heading west through the willow grove.

After a few hours of following the road, Nora noticed that the beautiful willow trees were steadily being replaced by large oaks and scraggly conifer bushes. When she tried peering past the tree line and deeper into the foliage, the light seemed to stop only after a few feet before unnatural darkness quickly swallowed it.

"Have we reached the Deadwoods?" Nora asked after riding up next to Rylan.

"No, this is the twilight forest. The Deadwoods are five more days ahead of us," he replied with a nod toward their destination.

"But I thought the Deadwoods started at the

Wanderer's gap located on the other side of the twilight forest?" she questioned.

"That is correct," Rylan answered with a glance at the tree line to their right.

"So, doesn't that mean we're going the long way around when we could simply just cut through the forest?" she asked, confused.

"The forest is a maze of monsters and danger," Rylan answered, still staring at the tree line. "We'd be more likely to die or get eaten than make it through. Even if we survived, there's no telling how long it would take to make it through."

"I see," she replied.

"However, we're making good time," he said with a glance toward the noonday sun.

"Really?" Nora asked with a tinge of hope.

"Oh yeah, we've already passed through Willow Grove. On foot, that would normally take three days running," he responded with a smile.

"Wow! These horses must be fast," she said, with an admiring look at the beast between her legs.

"Actually, that would be my doing," Gus said as he turned around in his saddle. "I've been feeding them a healthy dosage of haste." He produced a large glass bottle from within the confines of his coat and held it out so they could see its contents. Inside the bottle was a very clear liquid with an oil-like sheen to it. The liquid itself had a strange consistency. It appeared to stick to the sides of the glass as the horse's galloping jostled it around.

"I've been giving them a few spoonfuls with their oats," he said as he put the bottle back in his coat.

"Wonderful idea, Gus! We'll be there in no time,"

shouted Rylan as he commanded his horse into a run, galloping past both of them.

With a childish grin, Gus sent his horse running as well, chasing after Rylan, leaving her alone with Burnie, who was smiling just as widely as Gus.

"Come on, we can't let them get away," Burnie said with a chortle, spurring his horse.

Basking in the moment's fun, Nora hastened her steed into a deadsprint as she tried to catch up with the others.

Nora couldn't tell how far they raced along the road. However, when they stopped, she could see they had left Willow Grove far behind them. She wondered why more people didn't give their horses haste when embarking on a long journey. Soon after, she noticed the road was now hugging the edge of the twilight forest. She began seeing shapes of things weaving their way through the darkness, monitoring them. Perhaps that's the reason Rylan kept glancing toward the forest while talking earlier. Either that or something completely unrelated. Regardless, this sight sent a shiver down her spine.

"You see them too, don't you?" asked a voice over her shoulder. With a slight jump, she turned to see Burnie leaning next to her ear, staring into the forest's dark depths.

"What are they?" she asked while following one with her eyes; it seemed to keep pace with her.

"Those are the people of the forest; Blights," he answered. As he talked, the trees seemed to rustle their leaves in response.

"Blights?" she inquired, as the shadow she followed darted away briefly before revealing itself again.

"Ancient sentient beings made of animated plants.

They don't mind us humans much, so long as we stay out of their way and don't hurt their forest," he replied with a bit of a hush to his voice.

"So why are they watching us?" Nora asked as the sunlight seemed to dim a bit. A cool, light breeze racked her skin.

"I don't know, but it can't be anything good," he said, then hastened to catch up next to Rylan.

The fun was now replaced by a watchful presence. Nora kept quiet, as did the rest of her new friends, while they continued down the road. Now and then, a shadowy Blight would step up close to the edge of the darkness. She could barely make out a bark-like face staring them down, only to fade away into the darkness not long after.

That night, they set up camp on the other side of the road, away from the forest. Rylan offered to take the first watch as they unloaded their things. He took his sentry to the side of the road after undoing his saddlebag and grabbing his bedroll. As they built the fire and night set upon them, Nora could see that Rylan hadn't moved once since they set up the camp. Standing up from her spot by the fire, she walked over to him with a bowl of soup that Burnie and Gus had made for everyone.

"Are you okay?" Nora asked while placing the bowl next to him. Rylan was clearly on edge. This was not the carefree knight she knew back in the city; this was a soldier guarding his post diligently.

"I'm fine," he answered in a near-monotone voice.

As she looked at him, she noticed his hand lightly resting on his sword, tense. But what really told her something was wrong were his eyes. They couldn't stand still for one second. They darted back and forth, almost like they were chasing some imaginary creature. Reaching out, she tried to place her hand on Rylan's shoulder to comfort him, but Burnie snatched her hand out of the air before she could.

"I wouldn't do that right now," he said and drew her away from Rylan and over toward the campfire. "He'd likely attack you without meaning to. He's that jumpy."

"I don't understand," she said, staring back at the still form of her friend. "What's wrong with him?"

"Nothing is wrong really," answered Gus from the other side of the campfire, "he just gets that way when he's guarding the camp. He has a habit of blocking everybody out and focusing on everything else."

"Does he always do that?" she inquired as Burnie handed her a bowl of soup.

"Oh yeah, I think they beat it into him during his training in the northern kingdoms," he answered while sitting down again. "They're known to be quite brutal up there."

"It's no wonder he defected," Gus said, casually stirring his soup to cool it off. "I remember when he first arrived…"

She smiled and sat down next to Gus.

"He looked like he had gone through hell."

"In a way, he had," Burnie replied with a gulp from his bowl. "You see, the kingdom of Forstye doesn't just let their soldiers leave. They're too dangerous and too valuable to lose into the hands of other kingdoms. So, instead, they make them docile and inoperative through a process called 'Fire Branding'. This process is so painful, so brutal, and so efficient that anybody who goes through it loses themself. They're never the same again. Rylan, however, is the exception."

"How did he survive it?" she asked with a sideways glance at her stoic friend.

"He's joked many times, saying that dragon ale got him through it," Burnie said, finishing his bowl.

"My theory is that he drank chimera blood," Gus pitched in after setting his bowl aside.

"Isn't that stuff lethal?" she quizzed.

"In undiluted doses, yes; however, if diluted properly and administered in small doses, it won't kill you. You will, however, experience unbelievable pain, as if your blood is boiling through your skin," Gus answered while waving his arm around like a conductor with a baton.

"How would that save him?"

"If you adjust yourself to pain greater than what they inflict on you, you don't really feel it as much when it happens," Burnie answered rather sullenly.

"Sorry to ask. It's just that, in the time I've known him, he never told me any of this," she apologized to Burnie.

"No, it's okay. I honestly don't mind talking about it; but to imagine what he's gone through to survive, it's just not pleasant to think about," he answered. "Anyway, we better get some sleep if we plan to get up early."

"I agree," Gus replied after standing up. "Besides, the farther away we get from this forest, the better."

"Good night, Gus," she said as he made his way into his tent.

"Night," he said, his voice muffled by the fabric. Nora unrolled her bed and laid down on the durable fabric, staring up at the stars. How much did she not know about the world? About her friend? Compared to her companions, she was greener than fresh grass beyond the walls of the city. She felt completely out of her league.

She laid like this for what felt like hours, tossing and turning, trying to get comfortable enough to rest, but nothing seemed to work. She was too anxious. Her mind wouldn't stop racing.

She sat up, dusted off her pants, and walked over to Rylan, who still stood at attention. As she approached, she noticed he ate the soup she left for him and placed the bowl neatly beside his feet. Walking up to him, she tapped his shoulder lightly so her presence wouldn't surprise him. Blinking his eyes, his head turned toward her.

"What's up, beautiful?" he greeted in his normal friendly manner.

"Can't sleep," she replied while hugging her coat to her body. "Mind if I take over?"

"Not at all," Rylan said with an enormous yawn. "Call us if you see anything, and wake someone up within a few hours." He staggered over toward the fire where he laid out his bedroll, and after a minute, he fell asleep.

Nora hugged her coat tighter as a light breeze sprung up and slipped its way against her skin. She shivered as she sat down and stared off toward the forest and nearby road. With only the stars and very little light from the waning moon, the twilight forest seemed a lot more sinister than it did in the daytime. The trees no longer held any shape or form; they all merged into one dark moving blob of midnight, sounds of howls and shrieks radiated from its confines, and even the smells of oak and other aromas smelled soured and poisoned just to breathe.

The more she stared at the forest, the sleepier she felt, as if the very presence of the forest was hypnotizing her. Nora rubbed her eyes and stood up to try to keep herself awake, but it didn't seem to help. She wondered how long she had been up for and if it really was a good idea to take the watch after all. That's when she heard something strange. Turning around, she wondered if she had heard correctly given the surrounding sounds of animal calls, but then she heard it again, lightly drifting in the breeze. It was music, coming from the forest itself; soft and melodic.

Nora wondered if she should call out to the others. Suddenly, she felt herself losing her balance, struggling to keep herself upright. Her eyelids got heavier. She needed to rub them in order to see. Lumbering as fast as she drowsily could, she walked toward the campfire, trying to call out to the others, but to no use. All that came out was a line of incoherent mumbling. On her next step forward, she lost her footing and fell face-first onto the ground.

Nora wondered why the fall didn't wake her, why could she still hear the music, and why she smelled wood and earth all around her. There wasn't enough time or enough strength left in her to figure it out. She fell asleep instantly.

Chapter 3

Alex woke up, rubbing the sleep from his eyes. The sound of AC-DC's Back in Black told him it was time to start the day. Sliding out of bed, landing feet first on the ground, he tossed on an old set of jeans and a t-shirt from his locker. He grabbed his toothbrush from his washup kit and walked toward the sink, only to smash his toe on something lying open on the floor. Cussing at the sharp sensation of pain shooting up his pinky toe, he reminded himself to take better care of his room next time as he reached down to pick up the culprit, his journal. He kept with him while preparing for Operation Venture.

Flipping to his latest entry, he scanned his late-night ravings with a quick glance, then placed the book back on his side of the table across the room. His roommate used the other half to store his computer and a few books. Alex had a printer, his laptop, and a lamp on his side, with a few figurines to finish the space. He sat in front of his laptop and turned it on. A notification popped up, informing him had mail. After he typed in his password, he opened the virtual letter to find that evening training had been canceled due to graduation ceremonies.

Alex smiled at the alert as he read the list of graduates and found his own name listed in bold. He spent months training for this opportunity, and the payoff was today. After graduation, the operation would accept him without a problem. Standing back up, he walked out of the room and into the tiny hallway, which also served as a restroom. A small door separated the sink from the toilet and shower.

Eager to get going, he brushed his teeth as fast as he could while being sure he still did a decent enough job to get rid of any bad breath. Then he opened the door to the bathroom and took a piss. Lighter than he was a second ago, he walked back into his shared room. After grabbing his old hair brush and hair gel from his washup kit, he brushed his hair back and then to the sides. Smiling at himself in the mirror, he walked toward his phone on the nightstand and noticed he had a missed call from his sister.

Knowing he should call her back, he pressed redial, held the phone to his ear, and waited for her to pick it up. He half expected her to be mad at him for not answering sooner; instead, all he got was her voicemail. Shrugging it off, he placed his phone in his pocket. His sister was a busy woman; if it was important, she would call him back later.

Ready for the day, he walked out into the dorm's hallway and went right to the exit door on his way across the training camp and toward the mess hall on the far side.

***

It wasn't until later in the day that Alex's sister called him back. Answering, he held the receiver to his ear and sat down on a bench outside his graduation ceremony.

"Hello," he answered as he heard shuffling on the other end of the call.

"Hey, they haven't set you up with a starship yet, have they?" his sister demanded on the other end before he could ask what she needed.

"No, but they mentioned seeing about getting me set up on the Andromeda initiative," Alex answered with a twinge of curiosity.

"Oh good, I have an even better assignment for you," she said. It sounded as if she was rushing to be somewhere. "I'll see you after the ceremony, okay?"

"Okay," he responded just as the call ended.

What did his sister mean by a better assignment? If things pan out, would he be a part of the colonist's militia? The only roles better than the Andromeda initiative would either be a member of a Pathfinder team or being granted charge of a ship of his own. Unlikely though, Pathfinder teams are chosen earlier in the year and are required to take part in special training. Similarly, all the ship captains had been pre-selected. Maybe she meant a promotion higher than his current rank of Private.

Alex was so engrossed in these thoughts that he barely noticed the other graduates already lining up for the scripted march to their seats.

As he quickly jumped in line, he decided to find out as soon as he could later, no matter what. Alex followed his classmates down the center aisle of the room, where they then dispersed into their respective seats. As they walked, big band music played, cameras flashed in celebration of a fresh wave of explorers, and awards waited for them on stage. He sat down, wiggling a bit in anticipation of what was about to happen; he would finally receive the title of astronaut.

Front and center stood a woman wearing a red dress and glasses. She approached the podium, decorated with a variety of microphones. A light tap of her finger against them produced an earpiercing feedback screech. Groans of discomfort emanated from the crowd as she gave them her thousand-dollar smile, waiting for the crowd to calm down before speaking.

She spoke briskly and clearly. "My fellow Americans, we are here today to witness the birth of a new age in space travel through the discovery of the Quantum Entanglement Drive. At this very moment, nine of our finest colony ships are being prepped for a journey into the great unknown, to discover and expand our horizons far from this planet we call home. However, a journey of this magnitude is not for the faint of heart but for the brave, the bold, and the extraordinary. We are here today to recognize these men and women for being just that, as they prepare to say goodbye to the green cradle of earth and hello to a new brave universe. Class A, please step forward when your name is called to receive your medals of accomplishment."

This process went on for a while. Alex belonged to class D, which meant they had to wait for about 200 other people before their names would be called. Looking around, he searched for any family members of his, hoping someone had planned to surprise him and would wave at him from the crowd. He couldn't find anybody in the sea of chairs and people. Soon after, his class was called to present themselves, bringing his attention back to the ceremony.

Alongside his classmates, Alex lined up and approached the podium in a single file line. One at a time, each graduate received a badge in the shape of a spaceship. These badges symbolized the colony's missions to explore the black sea of space. Although just a badge, they reinforced the illusion that our teams were special enough to go to space. As Alex approached the stand, he felt a wave of excitement wash over him. When he was nearly at the podium, a disruptive hand reached out and yanked him off to the side of the stage.

"What are you doing, kid? It's not your turn yet," whispered a man with blond hair. He wore a Pathfinder uniform under his blue and black jacket and gestured with a hand for Alex to stand next to him. "And why aren't you in uniform?"

"Sir, colonists don't get a uniform until assigned a colony ship," Alex answered as he shifted next to him.

"Nobody updated you?" the man asked with a look of disbelief.

"Update me on what?" Alex replied, confused.

"Can't be helped now," the man said. He took off his jacket and tossed it over Alex's shoulders. "That will have to do for now."

Hesitantly, Alex put the jacket on as he started to piece together what was happening. His sister must have found some last-minute way to get him on a Pathfinder team. Alex smiled and silently thanked his sister; she knew he had always wanted to join a Pathfinder team, and by some miracle, she found him a spot. Straightening his new borrowed jacket, Alex studied the insignia on the shoulder; a pair of wings adorning a sword, with a space shuttle rocketing around the sword. The badge of a team leader—the

highest rank in a colony mission, granted only to the best—
the badge of the Pathfinder.

"Like the badge, kid?" asked a deep voice next to him.

"Sorry, sir. Just different to see one up close," Alex replied, not realizing how long he had stared at it.

"I know the feeling. It has a lot of weight behind it, but damn, doesn't it mean something?" asked the man with a slight smile.

"No kidding," Alex replied, looking over at him. "What ship are you Pathfinder for?"

"Sorry, I skipped the formalities. The name is Morris. I'm Pathfinder for the Liberty," he answered, shaking Alex's hand. "Considering the last-minute nature of this, I'm guessing you have no idea what ship you're with."

"I'm Alex. Nice to meet you, sir."

"Thanks. You don't have to call me sir, you know," he said. Their conversation was cut short as a big round of fanfare filled the air. "That's our cue." He said, turning toward the stage.

Alex fell in line behind Morris and followed him up to the podium. Behind the president stood another woman holding a wooden box. They reached the line with several other people across the stage, arms at their sides. Alex followed suit and tried his best to look like he belonged.

"Now, we will shift our attention to recognize our stars; the brave men and women who have gone above and beyond. We have identified these individuals as the very best to scour, explore, and protect everyone who serves on these missions." The president looked toward the line of people behind her.

Alex furrowed his brows in confusion. She was getting ready to announce the Pathfinders. He was supposed to be just another member of a Pathfinder team.

"Ladies and gentlemen, I present to you our Pathfinders!" the president announced. The crowd applauded as the entire line took a step forward toward the podium, ready to receive their badges.

Wait, this had to be a mistake. All colony ships already had Pathfinders. They must have mistaken him for one since he was wearing Morris' jacket.

"The medals I present to you today are symbols of exceptional skill and ability. Take them and excel where others fail." She made her way down the line, grabbing a badge from the wooden box, and pinning it on each of the Pathfinders' space suits.

"James Woods, do you accept this responsibility?"

"I do."

"Mary Wong, do you accept this responsibility?"

"I do."

Alex scanned the stage for an exit before she could reach him, so as not to cause a scene of any kind.

"Tagger Windhlem, do you accept this responsibility?"

"I do."

"Chris Rider, do you accept this responsibility?"

"I do."

Alex's scan revealed a nearby curtain he could use to duck behind, but just as he was about to sidestep behind it, Morris' elbow bump him. It was too late. The president stood before them.

"Morris Freeman, do you accept this responsibility?" she asked, grabbing a badge from the box.

"I do," he answered as she pinned it to his suit.

She turned to Alex. A flush of embarrassment

released a wave of heat under his shirt collar as he anticipated needing to soon explain why he was on stage. Her eyes prodded him for a moment, almost quizzically. She opened her mouth and Alex braced himself for her to call him out.

"Alexander Kingsley, do you accept this responsibility?" She pulled a medal from the box and looked him in the eyes.

He couldn't believe what was happening. It couldn't be real. How? Myriads of questions flew through his mind as shock swept throughout his entire body. Somehow, his mouth moved. Everything felt surreal; as if he were dreaming. The words slid from his mouth.

"I do."

The president pinned the badge to his jacket and stood next to him, staring out at the audience.

"Pathfinders," she said with a sideways glance toward them, "we salute you."

Alex could barely react. His mouth hung slightly open as cameras flashed and people cheered.

"Close your mouth, Pathfinder," Morris whispered in Alex's ear, and he clamped his jaw shut as he tried to process what had just happened.

Chapter 4

As Alex walked off the stage, he saw his sister waiting for him in her business attire.

"So how does it feel, Pathfinder?" Mimi asked mischievously.

"What the hell did you do?" Alex asked with a laugh, still trying to move past the shock.

"What do you mean?" Mimi replied, fake-punching him in the arm. "You're an official Pathfinder. Like you've always wanted."

"No, I mean, how did this happen, Mimi? What did you do?" Alex asked in disbelief and an air of suspicion.

"I told you I had a better assignment for you on the phone," Mimi answered with a pout.

"Yeah, I thought you meant a promotion in the militia or a spot on the Pathfinder team, at best. I didn't think you meant becoming a Pathfinder myself. How did you pull it off? All the colony ships already have Pathfinders." His smile would not leave his face.

"Not all of them," Mimi explained slyly. "The Future Warfare Company has just sponsored a new colony ship ordered to head into the Black Eye galaxy, and they asked me to find a Pathfinder, which is you."

"Mimi, that's incredible!" Alex laughed at the unbelievable turn of events. "Thank you so much."

"You're welcome, sucker." Mimi rolled her eyes. "Now comes the tricky part…"

"What do you mean?" Alex asked. A flash of worry streaked across his mind.

"Don't worry about it right now. I'll tell you after you get acquainted with your ship." Mimi handed him an envelope. "Head to the Western facility once you're packed up, okay? Address is in the envelope along with a detailed summary of the mission statement. Don't worry, it's a simple colonization agenda."

"Of course," Alex answered, grabbing the envelope and looking it over. "I'll see you later, idiot." Mimi walked off into the crowd.

Alex still couldn't believe he was a Pathfinder. Of course, he had dreamed of joining a team, but he never imagined leading one.

"So, how does it feel?" asked a familiar voice from behind him.

"Feels good, Morris," he answered, turning around to find him standing behind him.

"Good job on the promotion. You must be really good to be chosen for the job," Morris said, crossing his arms.

"I guess. I'm just a little overwhelmed by the fact I'm going to be leading a Pathfinder team," Alex replied, looking at the envelope in his hand again.

"Don't worry, you'll be fine. Just take care of your crew and they'll take care of you," Morris said. He looked over Alex's shoulder. "I gotta get going now, but it was nice meeting you, Alex."

"Oh, wait." Alex undid his badge, pulled off his jacket, and held it out to Morris. "Thanks for letting me borrow it."

"Hey, you keep it, kid," Morris said with a smile. "Fits you better anyway."

Morris disappeared into the sea of people taking pictures with loved ones, leaving Alex alone with his new jacket in hand. Alex put it back on and re-pinned his badge. He looked out over the crowd in search of his parents, hoping he could tell them the news.

***

The Future Defense's Western facility was the size of a football stadium, from what Alex could see. Its architecture reminded him mushroom made of glass and metal. Two of the upper floors protruded out and hung over the pavement, while the central mass of the building composed the rest of the floors. Barbed wire and cement fences closed off the area surrounding the building. As he drove up to the main gate, he noticed a guard patrolling the perimeter with a dog. They were likely sniffing for threats, like bombs or trespassers.

It had been pouring for most of his drive, but as he pulled up to the gate, the weather began to let up. The weather now settled into a steady sprinkling. The guard pulled back his rain poncho, exposing his head.

"Good day sir, do you have business here?" the

guard asked curtly while scanning Alex's car.

"I'm the Pathfinder for the Black Eye mission," Alex answered, showing him the envelope his sister gave him.

"Head into the parking lot on the left and show this to the secretary at the front," the guard instructed after looking through the envelope and handing it back.

"Thank you," Alex said, as he slowly motored his way toward the parking lot to find an open spot, preferably one close to the doors.

A little wet from the rain, Alex walked inside and took in the stark white and grey interior of the building. The design kept with the company's namesake. The main hall was an open, slightly humid area. He made his way toward the lady seated behind a long white table. She wore a grey dress with her blond hair pulled back. She tapped at some hidden keyboard and looked at her holographic computer monitor. Presumably, the secretary he had been instructed to speak to.

"Hello sir," she said as Alex approached the table. "How can I assist you today?"

"Hello, I'm here to see the Black Eye Mission. I mean, I'm a part of the mission. They told me to come here as soon as I finished packing," Alex said, stumbling over his words.

"Do have your registration papers?" she asked after typing something into the keyboard.

"Just this," Alex answered, handing her the envelope from before.

Looking over the contents, her eyes widened. Glancing over at him, she quickly typed a command into her keyboard. "So sorry sir, they expect you on floor B." She handed him back the envelope. "Just take the elevator to your right behind me."

"Thank you," Alex said with a pause. He took the envelope and walked around her table in the elevator's direction.

As he walked toward the elevators, Alex noticed that this area, which by design probably saw a lot of foot traffic, was largely empty aside from a few decorative potted plants.

The roof was at least two stories tall and curved into an arch, giving the place a bit of a future art déco feeling. The elevator banks also kept with the theme. Art déco metal prints adorned the entryway of the elevator. He pressed the button for floor B and waited in silence for the elevator to arrive.

A news broadcast playing from a nearby speaker announced that the government was currently in the process of talks with the middle east over nuclear testing and the usage of radioactive materials. Alex grimaced at the sound of uncertainty in the reporter's voice. The Middle East had the backing of Russia and China, whereas the U.S. had a slew of European nations behind it if things fell through. Either way, he sure was happy he wouldn't have to deal with any of that for much longer, once he left for space.

When the elevator doors opened, his sister stood inside, waiting for him.

"Okay, that's spooky," Alex said as he walked into the square compartment.

"Not really. The receptionist called me when you arrived," she said as the doors closed. "I just arrived in the exact elevator you were about to take. So really, call it a nice coincidence."

"You know I don't believe in coincidences, Mimi," Alex argued as the elevator started to move. "Everything has a purpose, even if we don't know it yet."

"That just makes you sound weird," Mimi said, smacking him on the shoulder. "Anyway, we need to get you up to speed on what's happening, and to do that, the most effective way is to take you up to our science division and hope Dr. Schwartz can explain it to you."

"Okay, but I thought this was a simple colonization mission," Alex quizzed, as the elevator reached their floor.

"Initially, yes, but the company has another goal, as all companies do," she replied as she led him down the hall. "Fortunately, it's nothing that isn't already listed in your job description."

"Well, that's good, I guess," Alex said, as they entered a room filled with whiteboards covered in equations and papers stacked everywhere.

In the middle of this mess stood a man in a lab coat, speckled with what looked like paint, writing on one of the many boards.

"Dr. Free, what are you doing in here? This is Dr. Schwartz's office?"

The man turned to face them. He stood at about 6 feet tall and was of a lanky build. His brown hair, shortcut and brushed forward, matched the brown shirt he wore, which had a picture of a gear and wrench overlapping with faded print.

"Sorry Ms. Kingsly, but Dr. Schwartz switched offices with me so he could be closer to the landline project. He said and I quote, 'Fuck those second-rate union workers. They wouldn't know an open circuit from their ass,'" the man said in a light British accent.

"Great. Well, since you're a part of the project, maybe you can explain what's what to my brother here," Mimi said with a gesture back at him.

"Of course, I'm guessing that you're our new Pathfinder," Dr. free greeted.

"Please call me Alex," he said while shaking the doctor's hand.

"Call me Gavin," Dr. Free answered. "Now tell me, Alex, what do you know about space engines?"

"Not much. Just that the original ones ran off rocket fuel and were eventually replaced by ones that could bend the space around an object, propelling it at speeds faster than light," Alex answered while finding an open chair to sit in.

"Exactly! That distorted space is called subspace—the unfortunate part about it is that, while we can travel through it with the new space engines, we haven't transmitted data through it. So, thus far, we have not been able to communicate across extremely long distances without eras of time lag. However, we believe we have fixed that," Gavin explained.

"I'm guessing that your answer isn't a bigger radio dish," Alex joked, trying to lighten the mood a bit.

"Haha, no. Actually, we think we can get rid of the radio assembly entirely and swap it out for what we believe could be the first subspace radio," Gavin answered by pointing at a picture of what looked like a crystal ball with two Tesla coils pointed at it.

"Awesome! So, I'm guessing there is a downside to this," Alex said from his newly found seat.

"Unfortunately, yes. In order to install the prototype, we had to remove the radio assembly, meaning that you will have no way of sending us a message. Even if you could, we may or may not even receive it," Gavin replied with a saddened tone.

"So, what I'm hearing is that we'll contact home once we arrive or we won't," Alex paraphrased.

"Pretty much," Gavin answered with an agreeing shrug.

"Anything else I need to know? No other experimental devices?" Alex asked, a hint of skepticism in his voice.

"Just a new labor system. Unlike other ships which have full manned crews that take shifts throughout a journey to keep everything in shape, we'll be substituting with robotic drones to cut down on human labor," Mimi chimed in from behind him. "You won't have to deal with them too much and they shouldn't be very integral once you arrive."

"Understood," Alex answered as he examined the image of the new radio. "I like my chances. When do I leave?"

"Once you pick your team, which Dr. Schwartz should have assembled a list for you. We could choose them now," Mimi said from the doorway.

"Oh yes, he left me a USB drive for you to browse," Gavin said, reaching behind a pile of papers to what Alex could only guess was a drawer.

"Perfect. If you wouldn't mind setting up the interviews for us, Mr. Free," Mimi said, a little condescendingly.

"Not at all, Ms. Kingsly," Gavin answered as he walked out the door and down the hallway.

Standing up, Alex could feel excitement crawl along

his spine at the thought of picking his own team for the mission ahead. Anxiously, he looked at his sister, who was rubbing her temples like she was trying to ward off a nasty headache. He could tell something about Mr. Free troubled her, but Alex couldn't figure it out so far; the man had been nothing but helpful and a lot more reliable than apparently Dr. Schwartz was supposed to be. Walking over to the doorway where his sister stood, he tapped her on the shoulder.

"Right…sorry about that. Let's find your crew," she said, turning to leave, only to stop and look back at him. "I know this is all unconventional, but then again, we're not known for doing things the normal way, are we?"

"What's normal again?" Alex joked.

"Exactly," Mimi said, as she led him down the hall again toward their next destination.

Chapter 5

Alex sat in a large oval room with a similarly shaped table at its center. Wood paneling lined the walls with a large projector screen hanging on one side. But from what Alex could tell, there was no projector.

"Unfortunately, Dr. Schwartz wasn't able to complete the full list, so I finished it myself," Mr. Free explained from his seat to the right of Alex. "I hope you don't mind?"

"No, not at all. Nice going," Alex praised from his seat.

"Thank you. I tried my best," he said, tapping a button on a slide controller.

The lights in the room dimmed as a projector displayed a picture of the first candidate on the screen from an unknown location.

"Our first applicant is Jason Cripps, a small arms specialist with a penchant for explosives. He was the top of his class; he has two tours under his belt, and 78 confirmed kills," Gavin explained while handing Alex a folder.

"He's completely qualified for deep space exploration. I wouldn't want anyone else on my team," Mimi remarked.

"Unfortunately, it says here he has a history of explosive anger, is prone to acts of extreme violence, and has twelve charges of misconduct to civilians," Alex replied as he scanned the man's profile. "This guy is a powder keg just waiting to go off. He'd be more of a danger to us than to anything we come across. Who's next?"

"His counterpart is Daniel Lea Avada, a sniper specialist. Unlike Jason, he did not finish at the top of his class; he has only one tour under his belt, and 42 confirmed kills," Gavin said after flipping to the next slide. "However, he signed up for SWAT after his tour and has a pretty clean record."

"I like him. Who's next?" Alex asked waiting for the next slide.

"Next we have Joshua Lock," Gavin said. "He has five years of experience as an electrician, graduated from MIT, has hobbies in archery and swordplay, and no documentation of any prior offenses. Seems like a good pick."

"True, if he wasn't legally blind without his glasses, or out of shape," Mimi argued from her chair. "Honestly, not the best, but he's something."

"True, I'll keep him in mind. Who's next?" Alex said as he wrote Joshua's name on the approval list.

"Barbra Engle, air force pilot, proficient with most aircraft, has run 54 missions, and her superiors claim she is the best pilot they have," Mimi replied, reading from her dossier.

"Sounds excellent. Call her," Alex said, swiveling

around in his chair for fun. "I feel like a judge for America's Got Talent right now."

"Haha, I thought that myself," Gavin chuckled after flipping the slide again. "Our next applicant is…"

The image on the screen changed to a picture of an old man in a lab coat with greying hair, and thick horn-rimmed glasses. Alex heard a groan as soon as the picture flashed on the screen. He turned to find Gavin holding his head in his hands.

"This is Dr. Schwartz, physicist, inventor, and astronomer," Mimi continued, obviously ignoring Mr. Free's reaction. "He cracked the communication relay problem and has been training to go on this mission since its inception. I highly recommend you bring him with you, seeing how he is an expert on the device itself."

"No," Alex said, looking at her.

"What do you mean 'no'? The man is perfect for the mission. Besides, he's the only one who knows how to fix it if it doesn't work," Mimi argued furiously.

"That's not true," Alex replied, turning to Gavin, "is it?"

Earlier, in Gavin's office, Alex noticed that most, if not all, of the drawings and equations had some connection to the subspace radio. That, coupled with Dr. Schwartz's negligence to appear for the briefing and the interview process, led him to believe that, although Dr. Schwartz thought of the idea, Gavin was the true genius behind its creation.

"Well, I've worked primarily on the radio itself, but I don't think I'm cut out for space travel. I mean, look at me; I barely look the spacefaring type," Gavin stuttered.

"Maybe not, but you're the right person for the job,

and I wouldn't have anyone else," Alex countered, smiling.

"I won't let you down, sir," Gavin replied. Alex watched a smile wash across the man's face.

The next few slides presented more faces with a host of good qualifications. However, looking at his own list, he felt the band of misfits from the first few slides were the best pick for the mission ahead.

"Now, what type of equipment do we have access to?" Alex asked, turning toward his sister, following his final decision.

"You'll receive an arsenal of high-end weapons, M-Tech combat armor, and five Shiva Exo-suits to use as your team sees fit," Mimi said, reading through a list she pulled from a file. "We don't know what you'll encounter out there, so it's best to stay safe. Of course, you will receive your own ship and can explore the galaxy as you wish while assessing planet viability."

"Nice! Sounds like we're set for deep space exploration," Alex replied, standing up from the table.

"Good, I'll make the necessary calls to the chosen applicants and get myself ready for departure," Gavin said while grabbing the list of applicants.

"In the meantime, I'll check on preparations for the ship and call you when your team arrives, so you can get to know them better," Mimi said, standing up from her seat.

"Okay, so do I head out the way I came in, or is there another elevator?" Alex asked as Gavin walked out of the room.

"You'll stay at one of our housing units near the ship for security and convenience purposes," Mimi answered, opening the door for him. "If you follow me, I'll show you to them."

***

Three days later, Alex walked down a long white hallway to what Mimi had told him was a loading bay for the main colony ship. This is where his sister has organized his new team to meet. On his way to the meeting, he wondered how they would be in person. Sure, he had read their profiles during the interview process, but he had no way of knowing what they were like as people. Would they accept him as their new leader? Would they listen to him? His uncertainty was endless.

Passing through a set of double doors, Alex stood in an enormous bay housing dozens of small jump ships currently being loaded with supplies for the colony ship in space. Crates and packaged supplies lined the concrete floor of the transfer station, some labeled I.S. and C. What these markings meant, he didn't know, except that they sat on the larger pallets and seemed to receive the best care. Distracted by watching the small spaceport operate, Alex was caught off-guard when he ran into something.

"Oh, I'm sorry," Alex apologized, turning his attention to the long, curly, dark-haired man he collided with.

"No worries. It's all a little overwhelming, I get it," the man replied.

The man standing before Alex was about the same height. The magnitude of his curly hair may have added to it a little. He wore khakis and a green cargo vest with a tank top underneath. He carried a large case, which Alex guessed, judging by the style, contained a rifle.

"Indeed, it's just a bit much," Alex said, looking

around once more. "Can't imagine what it will be like when we finally get to cast off."

"Oh, so you are a part of the team too?" the man asked, looking over Alex's casual civilian attire.

"Yeah, the name is Alex." Alex shook his hands.

"Daniel, but please call me Dan. I'm assuming I'll be the team's sniper and recon specialist considering my skills," he said, gesturing to the case he was carrying.

"Nice to meet ya," Alex replied. The man before him seemed a lot more laid back than the ambitious profile he had read. "Do you know where the meeting is? I think I might be a bit late."

"Oh sure, I was just heading there myself," Dan said as they walked further into the mayhem of loading and unloading around them. "So, what do you do?"

"Not much, really. I graduated from the academy a week ago. Before that, I spent some time with a small security firm," Alex replied as they passed a forklift hauling a pallet.

"Really? What was your clientele?" Dan asked as a jump ship landed next to them. "I mean, if it's all right with you?"

"No, I don't mind. I worked mostly with high-security targets. I once worked for the eastern Headquarters of Future Defense at one point," Alex answered, remembering the long nights hauling classified goods to secure safe houses and smaller labs.

"Nice, so you had some time to get to know the company before they asked you to join," Dan said as they approached an area with a few chairs facing a projector screen.

"A bit, yeah, I guess you could say that," Alex

replied as they entered the small circle of boxes that blocked off the meeting space.

"So, these guys are legit, right? I mean, they don't have any ulterior motives?" Dan asked as they took a seat.

"I think so. I haven't heard anything to make me think otherwise," Alex said from the chair next to Dan.

"Of course they wouldn't," a voice chipped in.

Turning around to identify the source of the voice, Alex saw a man with black hair and glasses approaching them from the entrance of the meeting area. He wore a nice shirt and jeans and carried a satchel over one shoulder. Thinking back to the interview process, Alex recognized him as Joshua Shire.

"Companies are good at not giving away anything they don't want to say publicly," Joshua said after sitting down in another chair.

"Still, they have to be semi-honest with us; they are sending us into space," Alex replied.

"They didn't need permission to send chimps into space, they just did it anyway," Joshua argued. "Not like we'd be much different…"

"Not exactly. Chimps are widely different from humans on many levels," a very familiar voice interrupted.

Turning in his chair, Alex acknowledged Gavin as he walked into the meeting area. A woman followed closely behind him. From his horrible memory, he recalled she was Barbra Engle, their pilot, vaguely recalling her long blond hair and aviator jacket.

"So, this is the team I'll be working with," she said precisely, as if she was gauging everyone up. "Not bad at all. When they called me last minute, I was afraid I was going to get stuck with the bargain barrel rejects."

"Well, we are not exactly mobile yet, but I bet we'll pick up steam as we go," Alex reassured her as she took a seat next to him.

"Good thing you have me then," she replied, nudging his shoulder. "Otherwise you'd be grounded."

Alex chuckled at that; it wasn't high-tier humor, but it was still worthy of a good chuckle.

"Well, since everybody is here, I guess it's time for introductions," Alex said, standing up and looking at the people before him. "My name is Alexander Kingly and I'm your Pathfinder. Our mission is to explore the Black Eye galaxy, evaluate planets for human viability, contact alien species, and protect the colonies from any potential threats. We're going to be the first explorers of this new world. Additionally, we have a second objective. The company funding this mission has replaced all of our old radio communication equipment with a prototype and it's our job to test it. If it works, we will be the first colony to communicate over great distances within our new galaxy. However, if it does not, we'll be flying deaf. Questions?"

"Yeah, do we have any idea what to expect in this new galaxy?" Joshua asked while leaning forward in his chair.

"Unfortunately, no. Every ship scheduled to leave is running blindly into this. While we can see the galaxy, general relativity will render useless any information gathered from current observations," Alex replied while trying to remember the basics of his physics class.

"The dossier says they're giving us live ammunition for this. Are we expecting trouble?" Dan asked while looking over a folder that Gavin handed out during the introduction.

"Don't worry. I've never flown into anything I couldn't get out of," Barbra said with a smile at Dan.

"That being said, we still don't know what we'll be walking into," Alex replied, unsure of how to read their reactions. "I'm not gonna sugar-coat it. Everything there could try to kill us. We're going to be the aliens to this place, and we'll need to survive and adapt in order to secure a new environment for our people. I know it's a lot to ask of you, but that's the reason I chose you for this adventure. Every single one of us here is the best at something that others aren't. Alone, we might not survive, but together we just might pull this off. So please, are you with me?"

"I didn't sign up to sit on my ass and look pretty. Bring on the danger. I'm in," Joshua replied with an air of bravado.

"You'll need somebody to watch your back. Besides, I always wanted to travel," Daniel said with a thumbs up.

"I'm probably the most unqualified one out of all of us, but that's not gonna stop me. Besides, you need a sciencey person in case things go wrong," Gavin said after adjusting his lab coat.

"I've flown worse suicide missions. Count me in," Barbra answered after throwing on a pair of aviators.

"That settles it. Within the next 72 hours, we'll meet here for Cryo-sleep prep and begin our journey," Alex said, looking over his team four.

For the first time in a while, everything felt real. This was actually happening in three days. He would begin the journey of a million light-years, and deep inside, he knew he couldn't wait.

Chapter 6

Nora felt a bag of rocks as she attempted to stand up, only to find that someone, or something, had placed her in a large wooden cage. Looking through the brambles that constructed her cell, she realized she was on the edge of a clearing. A mass of figures pooled in the center. The figures huddled, rigorously swaying and shifting from side to side as though they were being held aloft from the trees like marionettes. She couldn't see very well in the dim light, but she could make out the leafy texture of their clothing.

She didn't recognize their speech. The series of creaks and groans, much like the sounds of a windy forest, were foreign to her ears.

Although she couldn't understand their conversation, she could tell by the intensity that they were in a heated discussion. A long, heavy howl emanated from the forest, interrupting them.

From out of the forest, behind the figures, glass bottles smashed into the ground, releasing clouds of smoke.

Just as the smoke entered the clearing, another figure jumped from the woods, flipping over the center of the clearing, where it launched something covered in fire into the smoke, which now hovered like a thick mist. As soon as the flames made contact with the substance, a gigantic explosion enveloped the clearing. The figure responsible landed on the ground with a roll and raced over to her cage.

The figure reached through the bars with cloth-wrapped hands and, with incredible strength, pulled the cage apart. A loud screech similar to a bird of prey sounded off behind the figure in front of her. This noise caused the figure to turn. Her captors in the center of the clearing were on fire and the light gave her a good look at them for the first time.

They appeared to be grotesque beings of wood and stone, twigs and mud. Their shapes, immensely disfigured as if they got their proportions from a funhouse mirror. Their eyes burned like two redhot embers, despite actually being on fire. However, the strangest thing about them was how they moved; they moved like a squid does in water, flowing from place to place while their limbs swirled out behind them.

The figure at her cage pulled a sword from a sheath on his back and hack through the side of her cage in one swift motion as he noticed the creatures regaining themselves.

"We need to go now," the figure said, holding out a hand and yanking her to her feet.

They ran into the woods at a dead sprint. She followed closely behind this stranger as she heard groaning bark and shrieking birds chase after them. As they ran, she had trouble keeping an eye on her savior, who kept disappearing into the forest's foliage and then reappearing in front of her, almost as if he was teleporting. Behind her, she heard whirring as a piece of wood whizzed past her head and embedded itself in a nearby tree.

"Don't look back!" her rescuer warned as he tossed a bottle of something shiny over his shoulder.

Before she could ask why, something erupted behind them, casting shadows in front of her along with a deafening thud. The impact of the noise tripped her, and she landed hands first on the ground. Her ears were ringing, and everything seemed to slow down. She looked back just as a creature lunged at her with its wooden claws, only to be struck in the face with an arrow. Before she could react, Nora felt a pair of hands grab her by the arm and pull her forward, forcing her into a run. She felt another arrow brush past her face, striking something with a deep "thunk" behind her.

She paused to look in the direction the stranger had instructed her to run and saw a familiar face. Burnie approached her and pushed her into the arms of Rylan, who yelled for everyone to take cover. Covered by Rylan's body, a ball of purple flame streaked through the air, followed by another explosion. The heat from this one licked her legs like a wild tongue.

"Is everyone okay?" Rylan asked while helping her up. "Are you ok?"

"My ears are ringing," Nora said, rubbing her palm against the side of her head.

"Sorry about that. Flashbangs can be really disorienting, especially if it's your first time," a voice from behind her said.

Her mysterious savior leaned against a tree, his hood

and mask now removed. He stood at about five feet, ten inches, and wore armor that blended into the very bark he stood against. His face was very fair with a hint of dirt, and his hair fell around his head in long, messy tangles.

"Thank you, Ranger, for your help," Rylan said with a slight bow toward the man. "What, might I ask, brings you to this part of the forest?"

"No trouble really," the Ranger said with a nod of acknowledgment. "As for what brings me here, I'm afraid something has recently stirred the Blights into an angry frenzy. I was investigating when I saw your companion in trouble."

"The Blights are in a frenzy? That's not a good sign," Burnie said while scratching a tree with a knife. "They're normally scared of people."

"Indeed, another bad omen considering they have taken to abducting people now," the ranger agreed.

"It sounds like this isn't the first time this has happened," Gus asked as he stepped forward on the uneven ground.

"Unfortunately, no. Other rangers have reported blights taking entire villages near the forest. Thirty people gone under the cover of night," the man said with a down-cast face. "We don't know what they do with them, which scares us even more than the abductions themselves."

"I was taking watch when something knocked me unconscious. I don't remember how, but I remember hearing soft music," Nora recalled as the ringing in her ears subsided.

"Night whisperers," the ranger replied while shaking his head, "seems to be their favorite method of abduction. They put everyone to sleep, then snatch them from their beds."

"That's fine, but why did they target Nora specifically? I mean, whycleave the rest of us alone?" Burnie asked.

"I wish I had answers for you, but unfortunately, I don't. All I can say is that she's lucky I found her when I did," the man answered.

"And I thank you for that," Rylan replied. "However, we nevercintroduced ourselves. I'm Rylan Harlow of the King's-Glaive. These are my associates; Burnie Irons, Gus Gorvac, and you already know Nora."

"Pleasure to meet you. My name is Mathew Mot, but please call me Mat," the ranger greeted. "May I now ask you why you're on the road?"

"We're on an expedition to explore some freshly discovered ruins north of here in the Deadwood, king's orders," Nora answered, feeling they could trust Mat. Gus cast her a sideways glance. Judging by his body language, he didn't trust the ranger.

"Ah, I heard about that. Although, why the king is interested is beyond me," Mat said as he walked from his tree and over toward a patch of weeds.

"The king believes there might be something of value inside," Rylan responded as Mat plucked some weeds and crush them between his teeth. "Is there anything you can do to help us?"

"Well, I can help you get back out of the woods," Mat said, spitting the crushed-up weeds into his hand and rubbing them together. "As for your ruins, I have a feeling they might have something to do with the Blight problem, so I'll tag along if it's not too much trouble."

"Lead on," Rylan said as Mat grabbed a tree branch and swung himself away from the group.

They rested very little while they tread through the

dense woods as Mat warned them before setting off. Every so often, he stopped to pick up some weeds to chew, then spit back out. It almost looked as if he were taste-testing ingredients for a soup.

However, that was the least interesting thing about their hike. What kept Nora's attention was how the trees seemed to keep them in perpetual twilight. Occasionally, there would be a gap in the canopy, but instead of bright sunlight, there would only be shadows, and the little light that made it through was very dim.

It took them about half an hour before they saw the edge of the tree line and the open road. The change in lighting was near immediate as they exited the forest, almost like they had passed through some invisible field, from the weak rays and dark shadows of dusk to the bright noonday sun. The change was so intense that Nora had to cover her eyes for a minute to keep from being blinded.

"Wow, that's bright," she said while walking onto the road.

"That's the twilight forest for you," Mat said, shading his eyes with one hand. "Great cover and shade in exchange for the true time of day. Now I'm assuming you guys camped nearby."

"I'll show you," Burnie said, leading Mat to the camp from last night. As she was about to follow Burnie, Nora noticed Gus had fallen back and stood in front of Rylan.

"I don't trust him," Gus said as she approached them. "It's great he saved Nora, but he has no business coming with us. For all we know, he sent those Blights to kidnap her."

"I don't understand why you're making such a

big deal out of him, Gus. It's not like he attacked you or anything," Rylan argued, giving her a look that said not to interrupt.

"You know the stories about Rangers. You honestly want one of them hanging around us?" Gus asked while getting up to Rylan as best he could with his short stature.

"Yes, Gus. I do for many reasons, not including that we now have Blights to deal with and whatever else the world decides to throw at us," Rylan answered. "And if he has any ulterior motives, I'd rather keep him close."

"Whatever! Just don't come to me for help when you find out he's a sadistic psycho killer," Gus said, stomping off toward the camp.

Nora watched as Gus went over to his tent and packed up his stuff.

"What's wrong with Gus?" Nora asked once he was out of earshot.

"He's just scared of Mat," Rylan replied nonchalantly.

"Why is he scared of Mat? He's been a big help so far," Nora queried as the others took down camp.

"Rangers have sort of a bad name," Rylan answered as he motioned for her to follow him. "People think there's something wrong with a man who hunts monsters for a living and lives in solitude. Because of that, stories pop up talking of ritualistic drinking of monster blood and fornicating with beasts, which is complete nonsense. They're just regular people who dedicate their lives to keeping others safe when the kingdoms can't."

"So, Gus believes the stories?" Nora said.

"Yeah, but the guy also thinks that squirrels are out to get him," Rylan joked as he mounted his horse.

"Good point," Nora said, mounting her own horse,

only to realize that their new friend didn't have a ride to follow them. "Mat, would you like to share?"

However, just as she said that, a walnut-colored steer with a saddle galloped from the forest and up to Mat. He hooked one leg into the stirrup and swung himself up, sitting nicely in the saddle.

"No thanks," he responded, trotting off down the road. "Cricket will do just fine."

Chapter 7

The next few days passed by with little to no event, thanks to the helpful watch and guidance of their new companion. Nights were the most interesting. Mat would instruct them to draw a line of salt around the campsite and then sprinkle a vial of something smelly on it. Nora later learned it was a deterrent against most spirits and monsters.

Nora, with time, could learn a little about the history of their new companion. Apparently, Mat had been born to a farmer with fields close to the forest. Through his natural curiosity, he learned a lot about it. After his father died, he had no reason to stick around and began wandering from village to village, taking odd jobs to get by. Eventually, people learned he could navigate the forest better than any skilled hunter, so jobs that involved anything to do with monsters or the like were associated with him. Eventually, he met a ranger, who welcomed him into the trade warmly.

After several days of travel, they reached the broken river, a conjunction of islands broken apart by the intrusion of the ocean. From here, they turned east, keeping the twilight forest to their right, in what Burnie referred to as "a dead man's sprint" toward the Deadwood. In short, he wasn't wrong. They spent the next three days on a murky trudge through the overflown banks of the river that created a marshy bog filled with mosquitoes and other horrible buzzing things.

***

Five days through the marshland, they arrived at the edge of the Deadwood. At first, it appeared as nothing but a haze from a fire, but as they got closer, it became clear that it wasn't smoke but leafless trees. Now standing at the edge of the wood, she realized the stories were true. The husks of dead trees, overgrown in moss, swarmed the area in densely packed clusters. The temperature had fallen as well, the surrounding area growing chilly compared to the spring and murky marsh behind them. However, the most notable thing about this place was the fog, an immense soupy entity that swallowed everything it touched, blocking any potential line of sight.

"The Deadwood." Mat said from his mount. "God, this place gives me the shivers."

"You got that right," Burnie said while staring at the tree line. "Why we had a trade route set up through it, I will never know."

"It was a detour from the usual trade route, but lucky for us, we have a good angle on the cave they found. We should be able to reach it faster than they did," Rylan answered as he got off his horse. "From here, we can walk."

"That doesn't seem wise," Gus complained as he

jumped down. "Wouldn't it be better to keep the horses with us?"

"I wish we could, but the things that prowl these woods would eat the horses for breakfast," Rylan said as he led his horse to the closest tree. "Besides, the cave is only a few yards from this side of the forest."

"And don't worry about the horses," Mat said, tying his horse's bridle to Rylan's horse, "cricket will keep them all safe."

They dismounted and tied their horses together, then in single file, they began their walk into the fog-drenched woods.

No one spoke for over an hour, almost as if each one of them hoped not to draw the attention of any ghosts or monsters in this area. Thinking back to the stories Rylan told her back in the city, Nora recalled the fog wasn't actually fog at all, but the leftover emissions of a precursor artifact that clung to this part of the land for some unknown reason. From the cover, she could hear growls and bellows of creatures, monstrous and deadly, prowling through the trees. As Rylan said, the walk to the cave was short, but it felt like hours. They had trodden through strange foliage covered with moist dew to reach the cave that stood before them. Amid the surrounding fog, the cave emerged as a black pit of midnight, threatening to consume any light cast into it.

"Why did we come here again?" Gus asked as they approached the opening of the cave.

"Adventure, treasure, fun…take your pick and move your ass," Burnie replied while lighting a torch and walking inside.

Following his lead, Nora raced in after him. Burnie

was right; their journey was about discovery, to unlock ancient secrets that could shed light on the past and aid the kingdom. The inside resembled a typical cave; with stalagmites jutting from the floor like spikes and water dripping from the ceiling, some even forming stalactites. At the back of the cave, a path dipped sharply down into the ground, revealed by the recent collapse of the wall surrounding it.

"Everyone, stay close! We don't know what we'll find down here," Rylan commanded. He walked up behind Nora with a burning torch. "If you see anything that could be of importance, report to Nora for identification."

"Also, keep an eye out for traps," Gus added as he conjured a blue orb that danced around his head. "We already had one person die while investigating this place. We don't want to add to the body count."

"I'll go first," Burnie said, poking his light down the dark path.

"Stay behind me," Rylan said, laying a hand down on Nora's shoulder. Shivers ran down her spine.

"Okay," Nora replied as Burnie led the way.

After the initial trek down the steep slope, the ceiling of the passage moved closer to their heads, forcing them to crouch to forward. This then opened into a large corridor with dusty metal and concrete on each side, and at the end of the hall stood the two metal doors the search party had told them about.

"Well, we made it," Rylan said, holding his torch up. "Burnie, do you see anything?"

"Looks like whatever killed the trader isn't here anymore. I'm not seeing a trigger either," he answered, crawling around on the metal floor, testing every inch that seemed out of place.

"With that being said, how do you suggest we get this door open?" Gus asked as he stepped toward it, feeling where the seam should be. "I could melt our way through, but that would take more time than I think we want to spend here."

"Not to mention stupid," Nora said, walking over to the side of the doorway. "These types of doors are normally heat resistant; however, they normally have a device that's used to control their movements. In this case, the device appears to be gone, but there should be an override on this side."

As Nora examined the exterior of the doorway, she felt her hand brush something loose. Investigating it further, a loose piece of siding pushed open easily. With the piece of metal in her hands, she tugged at it, only to feel it give way in her hands like wet paper, causing her to lose her balance and revealing a complex mess of wires she had never seen before.

"Well, that looks complicated," Mat said as he helped pick her up off the floor.

"Well, of course, it's complicated," Nora remarked as she kneeled in front of the wires. "The Precursors were well beyond us. That plus a thousand years of neglect and you have yourself a very problematic door lock."

"Can you crack it?" Rylan asked as he stood in front of the door.

"Give me a minute." Nora pulled a pair of cutters from her bag and snipped away at what she assumed were the non-essential wires.

"Don't these old precursor ruins run on some type of power source?" Gus asked as she cut a wire in half and attached it to what she assumed could be the power source.

"True, why do you ask?" Nora said, twisting two different wires together, hoping to spark something.

"Wouldn't it just be easier to jolt it with magic?" Gus questioned as she gave up on another pair of wires.

"Because you would have just as much a chance of blowing the mechanism apart and locking the door forever," Nora responded firmly after ripping into another set of wires.

One of these has to work, she thought as she stripped the strange covering of the wires and twisted them together. Looking at the few remaining wires, she hoped that one of these pairings would work, otherwise she would have to start from the beginning with a fresh pair.

Just as she was about to go for the next set of wires, she felt a hand pull her back as a bolt of lightning jolted past her, sparking through the machinery. Behind her, Gus stood, pointing his fingers at the wires as smoke from the electrical discharge plumed around his hand.

"Sorry, I got impatient," he said as a very loud, audible clank echoed around the corridor. The door shifted in on itself.

"You could have destroyed our only chance of getting in," Nora yelled, standing up and confronting him.

"Relax. It worked, didn't it?" Gus said as the door moved, revealing the room beyond.

"That's not the point, you imbecile," Nora argued. "You could have jeopardized the entire mission. What is wrong with you?"

"I believe that might have something to do with the many times I've nearly died because of amateurs like you," Gus retorted.

"Um…guys!" Burnie cautioned.

"Amateur! Let me ask you something. Do you think you're the only person who knows anything?" Nora fumed.

"Yes, because I'm the only person who ever stops to think about anything before doing it!" Gus responded.

"Hey, married couple!" Mat joked.

"What?!" Nora yelled, turning to see that the others had wandered inside the room.

"You might want to see this," Rylan said, his eyes locked on the contents of the room.

Chapter 8

Alex's first impression of the Cryo-pods was that they looked like something out of "invasion of the body snatchers". The many pipes that hooked up to the primary unit fed a slurry of juices into the primary system, which delivered them to the occupants over a thousand years as they flew their way to the black-eye galaxy. His second impression was that they were claustrophobic devices made to scare the living daylights out of their occupants as they're loaded in and the lid closes overhead. That's when darkness had taken him.

His dreams weren't too bad. Mostly, he didn't dream at all. *Just one effect of Cryo-sleep*, he thought, but the tides of sleep soon washed away it.

Suddenly, there was a rush followed by a pop around his head. Then his body fell onto the hard metal flooring. Groggily, he opened his eyes and found his vision was off, almost like peering through a fuzzy lens. His ears felt full of pressure and were about to pop. He tried to breathe but instantly regretted it as he retched on the ground. His body contracted, pushing out all the contents of his stomach through his mouth in a slurry of liquids. This caused the pressure in his ears to dissipate, and he could finally hear the sounds of his own breathing.

"Sir, are you all right?" a voice from the haze of his environment asked.

He couldn't speak. His voice felt like gravel as he tried to form words, which caused him to puke again, this time more violently than the last.

"Sir, it's okay. Just breathe."

He tried to breathe in and breathe out several times. He felt better as he did this two more times till the last of what had occupied his stomach left his body. Slowly, he tried to get his arms underneath him and push himself up, but it was no good. His arms felt like limp noodles, and his now-settling stomach felt like raw meat. Slowly, his vision cleared, but it didn't help. The light shining on him stung as if he was looking at the sun. He tried again, this time wobblier, finally achieving a sitting position.

"Sir? How are you doing?" the voice asked again. This time, he could make out a distinctly feminine tone.

How he was, he couldn't tell at the moment. All he knew was that he was sitting on a metal floor, his stomach hurt, his esophagus was on fire, and he felt weaker than a piece of spaghetti.

"I think…I'm…fine," he said, the words sounding rough against his ears.

"Do you know where you are?" the voice asked.

"The Black Eye galaxy aboard a colony ship," Alex answered as the effects gradually wore off.

"Um, no, you're not," answered the female voice in a concerned tone.

Not aboard the colony ship? Something must have happened with the Cryo-pod, he thought, pulling himself together, feeling like pieces of himself were blacking out. The pressure in his head had left, and his senses felt clearer. Looking up at the source of the voice, he saw a woman wearing leather clothing, not the standard medical uniform. Where was he?

"Was there a problem with the Cryo-pod doctor?" he asked, his assumptions leading him to think she must be a professional.

"Cryo-pod?" she asked as her blurry features came into focus. "I don't think so. It looked perfectly functional."

"Then why am I not on the ship?" he asked as he noticed they were not alone. Four other men in varying garb stood around him. "Where is the rest of my team?"

Alex looked frantically at the people he now assumed were his captors. He marked certain key features about each one of them. They were all armed in some fashion, be it sword or bow, and a few seemed heavily armored. However, he couldn't find a piece on either of them. Besides that, he noticed the style of their dress appeared medieval. He wondered if a renaissance fair had captured him.

"Um…the other pods in the room don't look like someone has tampered them with, so I think they're fine," the woman who stood in front of him replied after glancing about at the surrounding.

"Where am I?" Alex asked as he tested his legs to see if he could stand.

"I don't know. Honestly, I was hoping you could tell us," she responded. "Do you know who you are?"

"My name is Alexander Kingsly," Alex answered,

shifting his weight to his feet and standing up shakily. "Can I ask who you are and why you are in a highly secured facility?"

"Oh, my name is Nora Hemlock," she answered, backing away from him a bit as he towered over her. "As for this being a secure facility, it is actually a bunch of ruins."

"Ruins? Impossible!" he exclaimed, pulling himself together. He tried to take a step toward one of the other pods, only to trip and catch himself.

"She's right," said a male voice behind him, "we had to blow the door's mechanism in order to get in here."

They can't be right. This was some type of training—some game being played on him to test his endurance. That's when he remembered the Cryo-pod; they often displayed timers so that doctors could assess the range of effects a long sleeper would experience compared to a short sleeper. These devices couldn't be tampered with.

Turning around, he hobbled his way to the side of the pod. With shaky hands, he undid the instrument cover panel, revealing the status of the person inside. As he pressed a button on the side of the analog dial screen, found the timer setting, and confirmed his selection. The screen beeped for five seconds before displaying the years of activation: 1,010.

Slowly backing away from the beeping screen, Alex turned to look at the people in front of him.

"What year is it?" he asked, after turning the question over in his mind for a few seconds. "1010 A.R.," the person wearing an eye patch answered.

"Or in the old calendar, it's the year 3033," the lady said, gazing at him intently.

Hobbling as fast as he could across the room, Alex threw himself on top of the nearest Cryo-pod. The Cryo-pods were not built to sustain life that long. They were only supposed to last the trip to the black eye galaxy. Any time longer than that could cause serious medical complications. The techie told him that, in theory, the occupant could survive for extended periods of time if hooked up to a Cryo-pod bay. Scrambling at the control panel, he shakily turned it on and searched the directory for the release function.

"Help me!" Alex pleaded, turning to the people in the room. "Help me get them open!"

He turned back to the faded screen and confirmed his selection, releasing a nearby pod that deposited the body of Gavin onto the ground with a soaking splat. As soon as he heard Gavin puking, he stumbled over to the next pod where the mystery lady tried desperately to rip into the side with a metal implement.

"What are you doing?" Alex asked as he pulled back the status panel. "Use the panels, otherwise you'll kill them."

Alex didn't wait to see a response. Instead, he found the release to this pod and confirmed his selection. The pod creaked as it shook and dropped Joshua on the ground, who also spewed liquids from his mouth. Then he heard an alarm sound from off to his left and saw two of the people that found him tapping on the status control panel as the pod opened up, then seized in an electrical shock.

"This one isn't working," one man said. Alex ran over and tapped on the panel.

"What happened?" the man with the eye patch asked. The panel had become unresponsive.

"The system seized up," he said, putting his fingers

in the pod's seams. "We have to get her out of there before the residual electrical shock kills her."

With all his strength, Alex tried to get better leverage on the pod door and lifted. The eye-patched guy did the same, pulling from the opposite direction.

"Come on, pull," he said, straining his weakened muscles to lift the lid.

The lid creaked as they pulled. Alex could feel the electrical build-up as the hairs on his arm stood on end.

"Pull," he said again, straining harder, pressing his weight into the pod.

The lid lifted, sliding away to reveal the sleeping form of Barbra. Alex grabbed her arm and pulled at her uniform, swinging her out of the pod just in time. The pod's systems surged one more time, releasing an electrical discharge that raced through the machine in a flashy, sparky mess. As Barbra's body hit the floor, Alex noticed she wasn't waking up like the others. Instead, she remained unmoving, lying on the floor in a pool of fluids.

"She needs medical attention, now!" Alex shouted as he dropped next to her, looking for a pulse.

"Let me see," a man in a cloak said, hopping down next to her, ripping her space suit open, revealing her bare chest. "She's losing oxygen fast, and I can't find any wounds."

"Beginning chest compressions now," Alex said, beginning CPR on her.

"Pulse is getting thready," the man in the cloak said with a hand to her neck, "We are going to lose her."

Alex stopped as the man took over in his place. There had to be a medical kit they could use or something to shock her back to life. That's when he looked over at the crackling, malfunctioning pod and an idea crossed his mind.

"Quick. Help me get her up," Alex said, lifting under her arms and dragging her over. "When I say so, we are going to lean her back onto the pod and then pull her away really fast."

"What about us? We'll get shocked as well," the man asked as they readied her.

"No time," Alex said, looking at the sparking shell. "Now!"

In one swift motion, they dropped Barbra's limp body on the pod. A loud electrical shock visibly ran through her body and she jolted back to life painfully. As fast as they could, they pulled her off the electrical hazard, feeling the electricity race up their arms in a painful arc as they all fell away from the pod.

"What just happened?" Alex heard Barbra say from on top of him.

"Redneck defibrillation," Alex said breathlessly, "free of charge, by yours truly."

"Thanks," Barbra said, "could you please give me your jacket?"

"Oh…Oh yeah, sure," he replied, taking his jacket off and placing it over her shoulders.

"Thank you again," Barbra said, zipping up the jacket

Standing back up, albeit unsteadily due to the shock his nervous system just took, Alex took a quick headcount as his teammates vacated their bodies of the liquids used that sustained them during Cryo-stasis. Daniel seemed to recover the quickest from the ordeal. He slowly sat up with a dazed look on his face.

"Are we there yet?" Dan asked, rubbing his temples, more than likely trying to relieve the pressure he had felt when he woke up.

"Not exactly," Alex said, walking over to him and offering him a hand up. "We're a bit off course."

"Hey, this is still the Cryo-bay," he heard Gavin state. "Did they forget to load us up or something?"

"More like something," Alex responded as he helped Dan get to his feet.

Turning to look at the mysterious band in curious garb, Alex noticed they were all staring at his group intently. Two of them looked almost critical, while another seemed lost by what was going on. The ones wearing some type of leather and chainmail stared in awe like they couldn't believe their eyes. Deciding to formally thank them, Alex patted Dan on the back and walked over to stand in front of the people who had saved them from their inevitable death by sleep.

As Alex walked over to these people, he quickly pieced together what had happened. They had slept vastly beyond their pods' expiration date and were currently in a broken-down facility. That, coupled with what he knew, meant that they arrived in the new galaxy, but some ca-tastrophe occurred that left him and his team in a new world to be found only now by a recon team.

"Thank you for your assistance and for waking me from the Cryopod…" Alex began in his best professional tone of voice. "Had you not woken us up when you did, there is no telling what might have become of us. That being said, we would like to be directed to the nearest medical facility for examinations to conclude there will be no further complications, health-wise."

"You're very welcome," one man said. "As for a medical facility, the nearest place is about fifteen days away."

"What do you mean? Did you not arrive via aircraft or land rider?" Alex asked, a little confused. *Were all conventional forms of transport lost on the journey? If so, the catastrophe that left them in their current condition must have been pretty bad to have lost the transport loading bay and part of the hibernation bay.*

"I have no idea what either of those things are, but we have horses tied up outside of the forest," the man said with a quizzical look.

"Okay, how do you transport back to the Nexus station?" Alex asked, curiously. Something is definitely odd about these people. How did they commute between the planet and the Nexus station they set up in the galaxy? It would have been essential to set up a market system to acquire the needed provisions and supplies from other planets and gain more settlers.

"I don't think you understand the situation here," the woman who helped him spoke up. "This is not the Black Eye galaxy, this is Earth in the milky way galaxy."

"That's impossible. We were to be loaded onto the colony ship Omega. Our orders were to colonize and explore the new galaxy," Alex replied as he went over their directive, "May I please link up to your Holo-chip? Maybe then I can sort this out."

"We don't have anything like that," the hooded man said, puzzled.

"What do you mean? Everyone has one. I remember they replaced cell phones, and I was quite disappointed with it for a while." Alex laughed. It was then, after looking at their faces, he realized they had no idea what he meant. "You have them, right?"

"We have nothing like that," the man with an eye patch said. "I don't think we've ever had anything like that."

"You mean you don't have anything like this?" Alex said as he swiped two fingers across his left forearm. An orange holographic display appeared, hovering over his arm.

When he activated his Holo-chip, he watched as a few of them stepped back, hesitantly, while a few of them leaned closer to his arm to see.

"What does it do?" the woman asked, looking over his arm with curiosity. She mentioned her name earlier, but he always had a hard time remembering them; he was better at recognizing faces.

"Obviously, it's some type of magical enhancement. Look at the color," a man with huge eyebrows and a hat to match argued. "I'd bet it's some kind of spellbook."

"No, it's not magic at all. It's just a Holo-chip," Alex replied as realization dawned on him. "Don't you have advanced technology?"

"We have simple machines but nothing like that," the woman said, stepping back. "Don't you know where you are?"

"I was actually just about to ask about that," a voice said behind him. During their conversation, Gavin had recovered and was wobbly walking toward them.

"You're in a cave in the dead forest in the Kingdom of Cerana," the man with the intricate armor answered.

"Cool, cool, but on what planet?" Joshua asked.

"This is the planet earth," the man answered again,

obviously confused by the question.

Earth? They were still on earth? That's unbelievable! What happened? Did they forget us? Turning to look at Joshua, Alex recognized the same line of questioning running through his head as well.

What happened? They needed answers, and these people didn't have them.

"Do you have any kind of information collection about what happened all those years ago?" Alex asked, trying to generalize his speech, so it didn't include any technological terms, which he was sure would go right over these people's heads.

"We don't have a lot of records or knowledge about that time, considering everything we know is based on ruins and fragments. However, there is a small section in the city library that might be of some help," the woman replied.

"Thank you. That could be helpful. Tell me, are there any other ruins around here that might be of interest?" Alex asked. He hoped they would find more information at one of these sites.

"There is The Crypt in the city close by, but the only thing I can think of is the Forgotten City that's supposed to be hidden below the floating islands. That's about a seven day trek from here, heading east," the hooded man said with a thoughtful chin scratch.

"And that's the closest?"

"Yes, but I wouldn't recommend going there. Nobody ever comes out alive," the man said.

Alex nodded to Joshua, who began collecting directions from the man. "Thank you for the help," Alex said. He turned to look at the rest of his crew.

Gavin looked to have mostly gotten himself together at this point. He busied himself examining Barbra, who was lying on her side, obviously not doing too well. Daniel assisted Gavin before standing up and walking over.

"How's everybody doing?" Alex asked. Although he was fairly sure what the answer would be.

"Barb's not doing too good," Gavin said from his crouched position. "You may have restarted her heart, but the Cryo-pod appears to have caused some unknown complications. She needs urgent medical attention."

"Okay, how long can she survive before we find a medical facility?" Alex asked, staring at the trembling figure of Barbra.

"Without medical attention and based only on the limited information from my Holo-chip's portable examination feature, I'd give her between one to seven days. Why? What's wrong?" Gavin answered after a quick check of his Holo-chip.

"Got it," Joshua said, stepping into Alex's field of view.

"Okay, so here's what we know," Alex began, staring at the faces of his team. "According to our pods, we've been in Cryo-sleep for over a thousand years; more than enough time for us to have made the journey."

"That would explain why Barbra is so fucking sick; these pods can't support a person for that long. I'm surprised no one else is in her state," Gavin commented with a hand gesture toward the Cryopods.

"However, we're not in the Black Eye galaxy as intended. We never left earth. Something happened, and we were forgotten until these people came along," Alex continued. "At this moment, we have one objective; we need to find out what happened."

"This just keeps getting better and better," Daniel said, scratching his head.

"I still don't see why any of this is a problem. We're a thousand years into the future; shouldn't they have instant teleportation and ray guns?" Gavin asked. Barbra coughed uncontrollably in the background.

"Unfortunately, we're not that lucky," Joshua answered. "It seems technology has regressed."

"By how much?" Dan asked.

"Medieval era, I think," Joshua responded, with a hint of uncertainty in his voice.

"Oh great, I'm going to be labeled as some sort of heretic," Gavin said.

"Either way, we need to find out what happened. We have two potential leads, meaning we need to split up," Alex said, presenting his plan.

"Are you sure it's a good idea? We barely know anything about this world and we don't have any equipment," Dan asked.

"I know it's not in our best interest to split up, but with Barbra in need of medical attention, one of us has to go with her to the city, not only to ensure she makes it but also so we can access the library for info," Alex said. "Dan, I would like for you to go with Barbra and send word back when you've made it there."

"You've got it. I'll make sure she gets help fast," Dan said as he knelt down next to Barbra and tried helping her to her feet.

"The rest of us will head to a place called the Forgotten City. According to our rescuers, it's the only place close enough that might hold any answers to our strange positions. If not, we might at least find some useable gear," Alex said, relaying his plan in the most convincing way for his team.

"So why am I going?" Gavin asked. "I feel I would be better off with Barbra."

"Simple. We need a tech wiz should we encounter any locked doors or broken tech," Alex replied after helping him up and patting him on the back.

"Makes sense," Gavin said.

"All right. Joshua, let them know what's going on and see if they have anything they can spare for us. Dan, prep Barbra for transport. The rest of us will search the area for anything we can use," Alex ordered.

As his team went to perform their tasks, Alex wondered how they were going to survive if everything was true. *Was there anything left? What happened all those years ago? More importantly, why didn't they ever take off?*

Chapter 9

The first thing Alex noticed when he walked out of the cave was the ever-surrounding fog and countless bare dead trees. Their rescuers insisted they come out last after receiving the all-clear. Now, upon seeing the landscape before him, he understood why.

Alex casually adjusted the collar of his Cryo-suit. It was still a bit damp from the Cryo-pod fluids. Thanks to the scarcity of items in the Cryo-pod chamber, it was the only thing he had to wear. However, it wasn't the suit that bothered him, but the caution his rescuers were taking. They seemed concerned with the fog and did their best to avoid it.

Flicking his fingers across his forearm, Alex activated the analyzer function of his Holo-chip. He pointed his arm at the nearest tendril of the mist and began scanning it. After a moment, the screen on his arm produced a slight beep, indicating the scan was complete. Taking his hand away, Alex checked the readout. The results were a mixed bag at best, with several components and figures he had a hard time reading. At his best guess, it was a toxic residue of some kind, but he wasn't sure what it was from.

"Gavin," Alex called out, still trying to make sense of the results.

"What is it?" Gavin said from behind him.

"I can't understand this," Alex replied, showing him the screen. "What can you make of it?"

"Looks like residual radiation," Gavin deciphered after grabbing his arm, "but something is wrong. It's almost as if something else has mutated it."

"Is it safe?" Alex asked, after taking his arm back.

"Relatively so, I'd imagine," Gavin answered, touching a bit of the fog. "Just don't inhale too much of it. Who knows what this stuff might do to your lungs?"

"Don't snort the clouds. Dually noted!" Alex joked.

Dan came out of the cave with Barbra strung over his back in a firefighter carry. The hooded man, whose name seemed to have also slipped Alex's mind, helped them along. Joshua followed closely. Behind him, the man with the big coat and hat, who kept glaring at them with what he guessed was a mixture of contempt and condescension. The others all seemed to respect them with a type of awe and reverence only reserved for the rich and famous. The girl out of all of them seemed the most impressed.

As Alex looked around, he couldn't help but wonder what was going on in the minds of his teammates. They only met each other before the launch, which to them seemed to only be a few days ago. Despite that, the five of them had really bonded. Maybe it was the fact they were stuck together, or maybe it was because they actually liked each other.

"I'm sending Mat, Burnie, and Gus to transport

your friends to the city," said the man in chain armor. "Mat Knows a path through the forest they can use, which will cut the journey in half. So they'll get help a lot faster."

"Thank you. That is very generous of you," Alex thanked him with a nod of respect. "If you don't mind me asking, where are you heading?"

"Nora and I will accompany you to the Forgotten City," he stated matter-of-factly while adjusting a strap on his glove.

"Thank you for the assistance, but do you mind if I ask why?" Alex asked. He didn't have a problem with them coming along at all; what he did mind was the fact that they had volunteered without his asking.

"Simple. I'm not about to let a bunch of unarmed people wander into one of the most dangerous places ever heard of, even if those people are precursors. That being said, we should probably leave here soon. There are too many things in this place that might decide to eat us," the man said, ending their conversation as he walked over to one of his friends.

"All right, let's get going," Alex said, with a twirl of his hand as he marched into the fog.

The first few yards were the hardest. Alex couldn't see very far ahead of him. Tree branches long fallen from dead trees littered the ground. Eventually, the fog spread out more, making it easier to see where he was going. The going wasn't too hard since the ground was mostly flat, but as they continued farther into the fog, he felt a sense of dread creep up on him. Dread or the fact he was being watched. The woman couldn't seem to stop staring at him.

Around mid-day, Alex noticed the smell of a charred animal corpse. He felt so engulfed by the scent that he could only guess that it was the actual smell the fog gave off.

"That's gross," Alex muttered to himself as he stepped over a dead tree branch.

"Smells like a dead animal," Gavin said, gagging a bit.

"That's strange," the man in armor said. "The creatures here don't leave their prey alone to decompose. Too much competition."

"I thought it was the smell of the fog," Alex confessed, just as he accidentally walked into something.

Stepping back a bit and looking down at what he had just collided with, Alex realized it was the large body of some strange, dead animal. It looked like nothing he had seen before. Upon further examination, he noticed the dead creature was missing a good chunk of its long, feathery neck, not to mention that the blood from the creature splattered all over the ground.

"I think I found the dying animal," Alex said, kneeling down near the carcass. "Blood is fresh, so whatever did this was here recently."

"This doesn't feel right," the man in armor said, unsheathing one of his swords.

"Joshua, what do you got?" Alex asked after standing up and scanning the area.

"Fog is obscuring everything. I can't get a bead on any animal."

"Keep an eye out."

As he looked around, Alex noticed that the fog had dissipated around them, forming a clearing. "Anyone else feel hunted?" he asked as he knelt down and grabbed the closest tree branch.

At that instant, something roared from behind the fog, followed by the pounding of feet. Turning toward where the sound came from, Alex saw what looked like a giant fleshy ape on two legs come charging at him. Pivoting on his heel, he jumped out of the way as its big meaty arm slashed at the ground by his feet. Landing on his butt, Alex quickly stood up, grabbed a tree branch, and swung at the face of the beast.

Twisting its head to face him, the monster caught the branch in its mouth, exposing long needle-like teeth dripping with saliva. Using the force behind his swing, Alex spun himself, flanking the beast as it yanked the branch from his hands. Out of the corner of his eye, he caught sight of Joshua fending off another of those things with help from Gavin, who punched it with his fists, each punch connecting in a stream of electric sparks. That reminded him that their Holo-chips had a stun gun feature for self-defense. Another ear-wrenching roar emanated from the monster attacking him.

Ducking, as the monster turned back toward him, swinging at him with its long claws, Alex swiped his right hand across his wrist and pressed a holographic button. Instantly, a cascade of arcing tendrils encased his left arm as he amped the stun gun's power to the highest setting. With a quick roll out of the way from another attack, he rammed his fist straight into the monster's exposed neck. Almost instantly, the monster's eyes rolled back into its head and it collapsed in a twitching heap on the ground in front of him.

Looking around, Gavin was still punching the other monster off of Joshua, slowly weakening its assault. Two more creatures fought the man in armor and the woman. The man slashed in a whirlwind of blades, staving off his beast's attacks, taking slices out of it when he noticed an opening. The woman, however, was struggling to fend off the monster's teeth as it pushed against an invisible barrier she had erected in front of her.

Picking up another branch off the ground, Alex leaped at the monster. He turned the long branch in his hands in mid-air, pointed the sharpest end at the thing, and stabbed it in its right eye. The beast roared as it dropped to the ground. Then, in a quick motion, it dodged to the side and raked its claws against the side of Alex's face, knocking him down on his back. Disoriented from the speed of the attack, Alex saw the other set of claws come racing down toward his face. That snapped him out of it and he rolled out of the way just as three cleaver-like talons penetrated the earth where his head had been only seconds before.

Thinking fast, Alex charged his stun gun, and just as the beast flicked out its arm at him, he countered the blow with a duck to the side and slammed his electric fist into the monster's armpit. The arm went dead at the beast's side. The momentum of its numb arm sent the beast rolling past him. Bellowing, the creature turned toward him and charged at him lopsidedly, using its other arm to gain speed. Bracing himself to jump out of the way, Alex felt his foot brush something, and upon looking down, he saw a knife. He quickly switched tactics, knelt, grabbed the knife by its hilt, and spun out of the way of the charging monster. And just as its head passed him, Alex stabbed the knife into the left lobe of the creature's head.

With his grip on the knife now lodged in the creature, the beast dragged Alex along as it slid on its side in pain. However, the creature didn't seem to be done yet. It began thrashing with its good arm and neck at the knife in its head. Alex knew that if he let go, the creature would skewer him alive. He activated his stun gun again. The remaining charge from his Holo-chip arced down his arm and latched onto the metal of the blade, sending an arc of electricity into the monster's head. The creature spasmed uncontrollably, throwing its limbs and neck everywhere as the makeshift weapon fried its brain.

The creature's body gave one last convulsion before lying dead on the ground in a tangled heap of limbs. Looking over his shoulder, Alex saw that Gavin and Joshua had taken down their own beast and were now busy making sure the beasts wouldn't get back up.

"Are you okay?" the girl asked.

"Yeah, I'm okay," Alex answered, wiping his hand across the new gash on his cheek. "I'm sorry, I forgot your name."

"It's Nora," she said.

"Hi Nora, I'm Alex," he said as he turned the blade in his hand and held it out to her.

Chapter 10

Nora felt ecstatic when she first met the Precursors back in the cave. As time moved on, she became a little concerned as she noticed how lost they seemed to be. But after Alex had effectively taken down two monsters with little more than the thing on his arm, a couple of dead tree branches, and a knife, she felt as if she was walking with legends.

After the attack in the fog, Rylan and Alex both took turns scouting the path ahead and checking their surroundings carefully. During this time, Nora bonded well with the other precursors. To her understanding, the one named Joshua used to be an adventurer. He told her many stories of his trips to different parts of the world. The other Precursor named Gavin was similar to her in the regard that he used science to solve problems. However, after listening to him, she soon learned that he was far more advanced than she was. She also learned that the Precursors never had the use of magic. Even the orange panels of light they could summon on their arms weren't magic, but simply a very advanced machine of science. This concept boggled her mind. Not only was it hard for her to imagine a world where one couldn't throw fire with a flick of their wrist, but also a world where science allowed man to perform acts thought impossible without magic. The idea seemed perverted.

It took them three days of fast-paced and careful trekking in the dead forest before the fog finally gave way, revealing a beautiful green meadow no more than 10 feet away from the tree line. They continued their march, at the request of Alex, till they were far enough from the dead forest that it no longer posed a peril by proximity.

As she gathered wood for the fire, Joshua swooped up beside her. "Here, let me help with that," he said, grabbing the wood from her arms and shouldering it.

"Thank you," Nora answered as he turned his gaze to the ground.

"Don't mention it. However, there's been one question burning in the back of my mind that I've been meaning to ask you," Joshua said, kicking a branch with his suit-wrapped foot.

"Go ahead. I've been asking you so much, it's only right," Nora responded as he hefted another branch onto his shoulder.

"Why are you here?" he asked while looking down at her. "I mean, I get that you're the closest thing they have to a scientist and that's why you came along in the first place, but after you found us, you could have left with Dan and Barb and gotten near the exact answers to your questions. So why tag along now?"

"Well, to be honest, the hidden city is the biggest precursor find in the world, but since nobody has come back alive, we have no record of any knowledge left there.

Plus, having a Precursor or three give us a tour of the place is something you do not pass up," she admitted in a way that made her sound selfish. She only realized it once she had said it.

"So, you are only here for the knowledge," he summarized as he walked back toward the camp.

"No, I didn't mean it like that," she said, flustering her words. "I mean, I want to help you as well. It's just a bit of a bonus to get to experience this and learn about your society."

"Don't worry, I was only giving you shit. To be honest, I only signed up to be a part of the Pathfinder team because I like an adventure. That being said, if you really want to help, can I ask you to go talk to Alex or at least make sure his face is healing? Ever since the forest, he's been pretty quiet, not as jokey as he normally is," Joshua said as they reached the center of the camp.

"Have you tried talking to him?" she asked, not knowing how she would help.

"Talking to who?" Gavin piped up as he lay on his stomach on the ground.

"Alex," Joshua replied with a look off at their patrolling leader.

"Ahhh yeah, we tried talking to him already, but he hasn't spoken up about anything. Seems to be bottling it all up, and that is not very healthy for him," Gavin stated from his spot. "I think he's beating himself up over Barbra. It's difficult to not blame yourself, especially when you're supposed to protect each other."

"No kidding, I keep running it through my head, wondering how it would have played out if I hadn't been puking my guts out on the floor—if there was anything I could've done."

"Yeah, same here. I felt so stupid and helpless, but Alex was the one who actually did the saving. That alone adds more to a life-or-death experience like that," Gavin said as he propped himself up on his arms.

"Where did you hear that?" Joshua asked incredulously.

"I read a psychological article before we left about the mentality of people under emotional and environmental stress," Gavin answered. "It was quite good."

"Well, either way, would you mind talking to him for us? Besides, he's pretty interesting himself," Joshua said as he gathered the wood for the fire.

Turning away from Joshua, Nora watched Alex walking back and forth while talking to the orange construct on his wrist. Gavin mentioned that the orange construct was how they communicated with each other over long distances, but to her, it still seemed a bit weird. As she approached, she noticed Alex had taken off one of his gloves and was biting the ends of his fingernails; whether it was from habit or nerves, she couldn't tell.

"Hi," Nora greeted, prompting Alex to turn toward her. His conversation was apparently finished since the orange construct that materialized on his arm was gone now. "Who were you talking to?"

"That was Daniel," Alex answered and then glanced to the south of them. "I was just telling him we made it through the fog and should reach the city in a few days."

"Wonderful," Nora said while keeping her hands behind her back.

Truthfully, she had no idea what to say to this person. He had a very inviting manner, but just by being near him, she felt he could kill a person with just a look. She also noticed a bit of a dreary tone in his voice when he spoke, almost like he was hauling logs on his back and hadn't dropped them.

"Anyway, he said that Barbra was doing okay and that they should be through the forest in the next two days," Alex replied while biting his thumbnail.

"That's fast. How did they even get that far?" Nora asked.

"Apparently, your hooded friend knows how to make it through the forest quickly," Alex replied while leaning on a branch he grabbed earlier during their trek through the forest.

"Yeah, he's a ranger. It's kind of his thing," Nora said with a chuckle.

"No kidding," Alex responded in agreement. "Anyway, what's up? You looked like you wanted to ask me something."

"I was just coming to check on you. You have cuts on your face," Nora said.

"They itch every now and then, but I think they're fine," Alex replied, pressing his hand to his cheek.

"If you want, I could try casting a bit of healing magic on it," Nora suggested.

"Nah, it's okay. Besides, I don't mind it that much," Alex said, then looked off into the distance.

"Something bothering you?" Nora asked. It was strange to see such a somber moment from a person she never imagined would have one; it humanized him.

"It's just that…" Alex started as he kicked a tuft of grass, "we've all lost so much because of what happened. Not only those we knew and loved—that was going to happen even if we had completed our journey—but we also lost the chance we had. To be cheated out of that by whatever random form of hell, I feel robbed. I can't even protect my own crew."

"Who did you leave behind?" Nora questioned. "My parents and my siblings," Alex answered.

"You must miss them?"

"Believe it or not, I don't," Alex said, with a hint of astonishment in his voice. "I know they lived good lives without me, and in truth, I hadn't seen them in years before leaving for this mission. In fact, I lost touch with my sister for three years before she called me up out of the blue and asked if I wanted to go to space. She got me an interview with the space program and then set me up as the leader of this team. If it hadn't been for her, I wouldn't have been here at all."

"Sounds like they forced you into this," Nora replied.

"No, not at all. I love space. Don't get me wrong, I love this job," Alex said quickly. "Nothing I'd rather do. I just didn't realize how weird the reality of it would be."

"At least you still have your friends," Nora said, looking over her shoulder at the fire pit Gavin and Joshua had erected, which now spewed a torrent of smoke.

"Yeah, they're pretty great." Alex smiled. "All in all, they're not a bad bunch to get stuck in the future with."

"They definitely like you." "Yeah?"

"Oh yeah, they're really worried about you. They noticed you aren't acting like yourself," Nora replied.

"Haha, I better explain myself to them so they can stop." Alex chuckled. "I wonder what we'll find in those ruins."

"Hopefully, answers," Nora said.

"That's exactly what I'm afraid of," Alex mumbled as he walked back toward the campfire.

As Alex left her side, Nora wondered what he meant by that. It was almost as if he had an idea about what had happened. Could he have already figured out why they were left behind? And if so, why hadn't he said anything? As she puzzled over this, an icy wind swept up behind her, causing her to shiver uncontrollably.

Glancing toward their destination, Nora could make out a weird haze on the horizon. According to Rylan, that was the ever-present clouds that encircled the ruins, forming an impenetrable storm barrier. She wondered how such a thing could exist in the world and how many more incredible discoveries have been left untouched. Was the entire world like this—wonder upon wonder, cloaked in hazard?

As she stood, she heard a whistle from behind her and turned to see Rylan had returned with some rabbits and was busy roasting them over the fire. He waved for her to come over and join them as he ripped a leg off the now-crispier specimen and tore the meat away from the bone with his teeth. Nora giggled at the scene he was making with it and walked toward the fire. *Whatever they would find in the ruins was a mystery for another time*, she thought. But the slight voice of anticipation whispered in her ear that, perhaps, they were not prepared.

Chapter 11

In the remaining days of the approach, Nora found herself spending a lot more time with Alex than before. She asked him questions about his world and the many wonders that he seemed to have taken for granted. Amazing things such as a tiny device that took instant pictures and horseless carriages were ordinary and commonplace to him and his team. However, there was one thing they all agreed was amazing; flight. But not just any flight she learned; space flight. They couldn't seem to stop talking about it, something they called the Colony Missions. Through this dialogue, she pieced together that they were supposed to serve as explorers on one of these missions. At least, before whatever events led to their entombment.

During one of these conversations, the dark clouded storm wall, which cut off the hidden city from the rest of the world, rose out of the ground and caused everyone to stop in silence at the mere sight. The clouds rose about 100 feet or maybe more and were dark as midnight. Constant surges of electricity that arched in magnificent strains throughout the swirling mass produced the only shreds of light.

"Is that where we're going?" Nora asked, staring at the nightmare that swirled before them.

"Yep," Alex said as he walked past her and headed straight toward the towering mass.

Throughout the day, the dark walls grew closer and larger as they made their approach until they couldn't see around the edges of the storm anymore. The sky darkened, and a chilling wind rose to greet them at the very edge of the swirling black mass. Torrents of wind buffeted them so strongly that Nora had to hold on to Rylan to prevent herself from being thrown around. The wind was incredibly loud, but somehow, Alex and Rylan could communicate silently. In quiet, they agreed to proceed into the storm.

As they drew into the vortex of the storm, the dirt carried by the currents of the winds ripped at their skin. Nora felt as if she was being skinned alive by the sheer force of it all. It became so intense that, within the next five seconds, Nora couldn't see or hear anyone else, let alone know where she was going. She clung onto Rylan's arm, her only anchor in this whirling dervish. It felt like forever as they walked deeper into the storm; the wind drowning out everything except for its monstrous gusts.

Nora almost lost her footing a couple of times as the force of the wind threatened to throw her into the air. After the fourth time, Rylan held onto her with both arms in a bear hug. The wind's power and presence felt endless, stripping at her hands and face like a grinding wheel of air until it wasn't. Opening her raw eyelids, she felt a cool breeze kiss her face. Structures rose from the cover of the heavy clouds. Below her, an enormous crater in front of where she stood on its edge.

"Is that?" Nora asked in disbelief.

"It is," Rylan answered from behind her. "Where are the others?"

"I don't know. I thought they were next to us. You can't see anything in there," Nora responded, looking around the edge of the crater.

It didn't take long for Alex to emerge from the storm wall behind them. His face looked red with multiple tiny, bleeding cuts. Over his shoulder, he carried Gavin, who had passed out due to the intensity of their trek. Behind him soon followed Joshua, who looked even more tired than Alex and then, consequently, doubled over in a heap, trying to catch his breath.

"What happened?" Nora asked, running over to help grab Gavin and place him on the ground.

"He walked into an air pocket and it sucked the air out of him," Alex explained as he stood up and wiped his face with the back of his hand. "He's lucky Joshua and I stuck back to keep an eye out, otherwise he would have likely died from suffocation."

"That's what those hand gestures meant back there?" Nora asked as she noticed Gavin come around.

"Pretty much. I was trying to say, 'Single file everybody. Hold on to each other,' but it still worked out," Alex answered. Gavin fell into a coughing fit on the ground before rolling over onto his side.

"Did we make it?" Gavin groaned at her feet.

"Yeah, we made it," Alex said, reaching down and grabbing his friend's arm, then hoisting him upright.

"Guys, look at this!" Joshua shouted from behind.

Turning around to see what Joshua wanted them

to look at, Nora noticed something looked off with him. In fact, his face scrunched up in a mixture of shock and confusion. Alex walked past her, leading Gavin over to the spot Joshua stood. The same look of shock swept over both of their faces in a mask of emotion, stopping them in their tracks. Going over to where they stood, Nora could see they were looking out over the ruined structures below. Then it occurred to her that this place probably meant something to them. Judging by the look on all their faces, this place had been important.

"Do you know this place?" Nora asked cautiously.

By the time she finished her question, Alex had already started descending the inner side of the crater in silence.

"Did I say something wrong?" Nora asked with a worried look on her face.

"No, it's not you," Joshua answered as he joined Alex's descent.

"This place used to be home," Gavin answered before following the other two. Lacking the physical prowess of Alex and Joshua, Gavin opted to shakily slide down the edge of the crater on his butt.

As Nora watched them disappear into the heavy cloud cover, she wondered why that explanation didn't make her feel any better now. "Hey," Rylan said as she felt a hand gently grab her shoulder, "you okay?"

"I don't know, Rylan. I feel terrible for coming here now. I mean, I knew they probably would know this place, but I never expected it to be like this," Nora replied, her arms crossed in front of her.

"Listen, it's going to be okay. They're just distancing themselves to process what they've lost. Don't worry, they'll be fine eventually," Rylan said.

"Okay," Nora said downheartedly.

"Hey, it's not your fault. They asked us to bring them here," Rylan said, brushing a strand of hair out of her face with his thumb. "Now let's get down there and see if they need any help."

"Okay." Nora nodded yes.

"Besides, we can't let them find all the good stuff," Rylan said as he slid down the side of the crater himself.

A slight breeze accompanied them as they slid down the side of the crater's edge. But as Nora slid below the cloud cover, the breeze stopped. The pungent smell of dead air filled the space. As she reached the end of her slide, she noticed the others had already walked forward down what she assumed was a road, although she couldn't figure out what material it consisted of. This observation didn't seem to bother the Precursors, or they didn't notice it, as they silently observed the surrounding remains of what had once been their home.

They continued walking among the rubble of fallen relics. One decrepit building, in particular, caught her eye. An entire side of it stood exposed, completely open to the elements. Within its rubble, something shiny caught some sliver of light and reflected back at her. Upon further investigation, it belonged to a piece of metal that jutted from a pile of wreckage. She pulled on the end of it and the pile of stones that previously the piece gave way and collapsed at her feet, producing a small cloud of dust. Turns out her find was nothing more than scrap metal, the reflection caused by one of its more pristine sides.

"You okay?" a voice asked behind her. Alex stood behind her.

"Yes, I'm okay," she replied.

"All right," Alex said. He turned as if to go before stopping and turning back to her. "Listen, I'm sorry if I came off a little insensitive earlier. I didn't mean it."

"Oh no. It's okay. I completely understand," she said hurriedly. "It must be hard seeing it like this."

"Okay," he said. He looked down at the metal in her hand and his expression changed. "Where did you find that?"

"Over in that pile of rubble," Nora answered as he grabbed her arm and pulled her away from the rubble as fast as he could. "What's the problem?"

"That could be potentially dangerous," Alex answered, as he grabbed the metal from her hands and tossed it away from them. "Guys, watch out. We have radiation hotspots."

"Radiation hot spots? What's that?" Nora questioned as she noticed a strange symbol, faded almost beyond recognition on the back of the metal piece she picked up.

"Hopefully, nothing too bad, but I wouldn't like to take the chance either way," Alex replied. He looked around them, searching for something, but didn't find it. He quickly ushered Nora over to the rest of the group.

They kept close together after that. Nora noticed the only deviation from the group was Joshua, who took point, searching ahead a few feet, scanning the area, and then continuing on ahead of them. Gavin, during all of this, tried his best to explain radiation to them. As far as she could understand, it wasn't good for living things. Time seemed to pass by like mud in here, Nora noticed that it didn't seem to get darker or lighter in here, but remained murky and grey at all times. Nora wasn't sure if the surrounding storm caused this or not; besides magic, she couldn't think of any other answer.

Nora was so wrapped up in her own thoughts that she didn't notice they had stopped moving and accidentally bumped into Rylan. They had arrived at some form of intersection with massive structures. Castle-like spires rose from crumbling heaps at each of the four corners. However, one in particular caught the Precursors' attention, and it was the biggest of the quartet, its structure made from mostly metal.

"What is this place?" Nora asked as the Precursors moved toward the building.

"This is HQ," Alex said over his shoulder. "If any place has answers, it's here."

With that comment, the group walked across toward a large open entrance and proceeded into the darkness within.

Chapter 12

As Alex entered the Future Warfare Department Headquarters, he realized how eerie it was with nobody walking around, no lights illuminating the room, and dust covering every surface. He had only ever been here once, the day after he selected his crew, as it was a formality to be congratulated by the CEO. Now, a thousand years in the future, there were no meetings to go to and no CEO to please. All that remained were remnants of its signature art déco style and concrete, a dark tomb of a time long past. It was too dark. Alex flipped on his Holo-chip and he held up his arm, shedding whatever illumination it could give on the dimly lit scene before them. Luckily, Rylan had his own idea and had instead begun lighting torches.

Glancing around the wreckage of this place Alex felt his certainty of those he'd left behind having lived long and good lives and a pit of despair began to form in his stomach.

"Okay, what are we looking for?" Rylan asked,

handing Alex a torch.

"Gavin, you know this place better than I do. Any ideas?" Alex said, lifting the fiery stick in front of him.

"Headquarters stored their data vault four stories down. If I remember correctly, that place should be pneumatically sealed. So, if we're lucky, everything should be well preserved," Gavin answered, heading toward a doorway that had almost crumbled in on itself with time. "This should lead us down."

"Any other way of getting down that doesn't involve the staircase of death?" Alex asked as he walked over and tapped the doorway with a quizzical finger.

"Unless you want to climb down the elevator shaft, this is it," Gavin answered with a look toward where the elevators would be.

"Okay, everybody group up," Alex said as they entered through the doorway. "Stay within earshot of each other and watch your backs. There's no telling what could be living down here."

"Keep yourself in within the torchlight as much as possible. If anything is down there, chances are it won't go anywhere near it," Rylan added as Alex began helping Gavin through.

"Yeah, he's right," Alex agreed, holding out a hand to Nora, who went through the hole next.

After pulling Nora through, Alex descended the crumbling staircase, holding an arm out to test the darkness with his torch. Alex thought the stairs weren't the trickiest thing to navigate as he hopped from step to step, testing each step with his weight. This kind of reminded him of when he used to play "the floor is lava" as a kid. He was about to take another step down when he felt the rock under his foot give way, and he fell straight down a hole as the floor crumbled beneath him.

"Alex!!!" Nora scream, but it was already too late.

The only visible thing below him was the all-consuming darkness. He reached out to grab anything to stop his fall. In doing so, he felt something pierce through his left arm, stopping his descent with a lurch that yanked out his shoulder with a tearing pain down his forearm that quickly followed. Looking up with a cry of pain, he discovered that he now hung on a piece of rebar that had ripped through his arm. He had stopped falling, for now, by the grace of his injury.

Pulling himself up with his injured arm, Alex grabbed the ledge the rebar protruded from and hoisted himself up on top of it. Once on the top, he pulled his arm free of the rebar, which was just as painful as when it went in. He grit his teeth as the shaft made a sucking sound while coming out of his wound. With one last tug, the rebar came free of his body, and so did a torrent of blood. Alex quickly applied pressure to the wound with his other hand. He laid his back against the wall and clenched his jaw against the intense pain. The others called down after him.

"I'm here!" Alex shouted back while using his free arm to rip off a sleeve of his Cryo-suit.

"Thank god. Are you okay?!" Joshua shouted.

"Not exactly! I'm going to need medical attention fast!!!" Alex shouted, tying the sleeve around his elbow and making a tourniquet to slow down his blood loss.

"What's wrong?!" Nora asked.

"A piece of rebar skewered my forearm and I'm bleeding badly!" Alex replied, putting more pressure on the hole in his arm. "Funny thing is, it actually saved me from the fall."

"Okay, hold on. We're going to find a way down to you," Rylan said, followed by the falling of loose rubble.

"No, don't. It's too unstable to go any farther down this way," Alex said after watching more of the stairway crumbling past him. "I think I'm a floor or two beneath you. Gavin, is there another way down?"

"There should be another set of stairs across the building. If not, we can try the ventilation system, but that might be even less safe than the stairs. We could also try the elevator shaft if we can find enough rope," Gavin answered after a quick minute.

"Okay, try the stairs first. I'll head that way myself and meet you there," Alex ordered while using the wall to help him stand. "If that doesn't work, then we'll try the alternatives."

"Okay, we'll hurry. Just hold on!" Joshua shouted as Alex approached the door to the current floor and opened it to the corridor of darkness before him.

The hallway stood darker than the blackest pit Alex could imagine. As the lights of his companions disappeared from the hallway behind him, complete darkness grew slowly around him until it swallowed him completely. Waving a hand over his wounded arm, Alex tried to activate his Holo-chip, but nothing happened. It suddenly dawned on him that it was highly possible the rebar could have removed his implant upon impact with his arm. Cursing under his breath, Alex slowly walked forward into the hall, waving his good arm in front of him, feeling his way and using the wall to his left as a guide.

Darkness swirled around him like a living being as he progressed through the hall. In truth, he had never been a big fan of the dark, but he had a habit of always conquering his fears the best he could. Now, being alone, defenseless, and losing blood, his imagination started creating shapes all around him. Alex got dizzy as he tried to move faster, forcing him to stop and lean against the wall and close his eye for a bit. He was about to start moving again when he heard a sound off to his right, coming from inside a nearby closed room. He pushed himself up against the wall and tried to stand as still as possible as he stared into the darkness that enveloped his vision.

The sound grew closer, becoming a breathy hiss. He felt the damp breath of something rear its head close to his face. Alex held his breath. Fear coursed through his body. If this creature had lived down in this darkness for so long, he figured that it would have developed some kind of mechanism to navigate without light. The calls of his companions from down the hall broke the silence as they made their way over in his direction. The sound must have scared off the creature because it ran off.

"Alex, are you okay?" Gavin asked as he approached with a torch.

"Holy shit! You did a number on yourself."

"I think it tore my chip out too, but at least it saved my life," Alex answered with a look at the ragged mess that was his arm. "I don't think I'll be using it anymore for a long while, though."

"I'm thinking for the rest of your life, just judging by the sight alone. We would need medical equipment we don't have and fast to even try to save it," Gavin said with a look at his arm.

"That doesn't look too bad," Rylan interjected from behind Gavin. "A good healing spell could fix that right up."

"No, it won't. We need bandages and a hefty dose of nanogel for this," Gavin argued, lifting Alex's arm and scanning it with his Holochip.

"Nonsense. Hey Nora, you know a healing spell, don't you?" Rylan said and then looked over at her.

"That's not going to work," Gavin argued, and Alex could see him grit his teeth.

"No, it will…," Rylan began before Gavin turned around and grabbed his collar, pulling him toward his face.

"Listen, I know you think magic is a thing and everything, but according to the laws of science, that is not possible in even the most extreme circumstances. What Alex needs is a doctor with advanced medical equipment that we don't have at the moment, because the world of science got flushed down the shitter somehow, and now we are stuck in this shitting nightmare of a world where my teammates are going to die," Gavin yelled at him with an expression of pure frustration.

While this took place, Alex felt someone's hands on his arm. He turned his head to see Nora, who had her eyes closed in a look of pure concentration.

"Nora, what are you doing?" Alex questioned as a bright green light seeped from her palms and into his mangled arm like a snake.

As this happened, Alex's arm itched; his arm soon stitched together, weaving broken bone and flesh into its original shape. Alex noticed that the arguing had stopped, and with a look over in Gavin's direction, he saw him staring at the miracle happening before his eyes.

By this point, his arm appeared nearly healed, with the last few patches of skin melting into place. Pulling her hands away from his arm, he flexed his hand and didn't feel any pain as he moved as if nothing ever happened.

"That's impossible!" Gavin exclaimed.

"My thoughts exactly, but it's real, I think," Alex muttered, looking at Nora. "How did you do that?"

"I've learned a few spells working as an Artificer," Nora explained with a smile.

"No, I mean, how did you do that? That is physically impossible," Alex said.

"It's magic. It's a very potent form of power," Nora explained in the best way she could. "There's nothing really to it. Some people have to learn how to use it like me, and others are born with it."

"That still doesn't make sense," Gavin argued. "You can't just wave your hand and fix all your problems. Life doesn't work like that."

"Magic doesn't work like that," Rylan interjected.

"What do you mean? If I can wave my hand and heal a guy, why can't I solve all my problems with a few words?" Gavin quizzed.

"Gavin," Alex said as he stood up, testing his arm. "I think he meant that it's limited to controlling certain elements and not to the very principles of the universe."

"Oh, that makes slightly more sense," Joshua said.

"Yeah, I guess," Gavin muttered.

"Either way, we have another problem. We're not alone down here," Alex said as Nora handed him her torch.

"What do you mean?" Rylan asked, glancing around at their surroundings.

"Right before you found me, something tall and lanky was crawling around down here," Alex replied.

"Hmm, sounds like a stalker. They're mostly harmless unless provoked. They're mostly scavengers,"

Rylan answered with a look around the area. "Still, we shouldn't wait around for more of them."

"True, would hate to have to fight anymore in our current condition. Gavin, how far away is the data vault?" Alex responded.

"Should be in the southwest section of this level," Gavin responded, looking at his Holo-chip.

"All right, move out," Alex ordered with a hand gesture as he crept into the darkness in the direction Gavin pointed.

This floor, without light, was essentially a maze if you didn't know where you were going, and the many pitfalls on the floor below made getting around a lot harder. However, with Gavin leading them, Alex felt it made the going a lot easier. After a few more left turns, Alex stood in front of a massive metal door, behind which rested the answers to what happened.

The vault door opened easily, to Alex's surprise. Apparently, a thousand years of wear on any lock could weaken its internal mechanisms. Once they opened the door, they stepped into the room to find rows of servers in a dark room. Judging by how it looked, Alex figured there was no power coursing through any of them. This didn't seem to deter Gavin, however. He ran over to a console and clacked away at the keys in a flurry.

"Back-up generators are still online, but there is no telling how long they'll last, especially considering how long they've been lying around," Gavin answered and looked at Alex.

"Then, let's worry about the pressing question first," Alex said, looking over at Joshua. "Why did they leave us behind?"

Chapter 13

All three of them leaned over the console's screen, scouring the documents that popped up from their search. Various types of documents scrolled across the screen, depicting mission parameters, navigation, schematics, crew positions, and Cryoprocedures; the full extent of the mission in a computerized format.

"I'm not seeing anything new here. How about you guys?" Gavin asked with his eyes scanning the screen.

Scrolling to the bottom of the documentation of events around the mission's launch date, Alex noticed that the log cut off after the Cryo of the Pathfinder team. Instead, a brief bulletin note hung right below it with the title "Project Morpheus" in bold.

"What's Project Morpheus?" Alex asked, pointing to the bulletin at the end of the page.

"Looks like they added it after our freezing, but I can't seem to access it. It's encrypted, and it'll take too long to decode."

"Is there anything else that might show what happened with the main colony ship, or any of the other installations?" Alex asked.

"Not really. However, it's strange. It looks like the system backed itself up soon after we went to sleep," Gavin reported.

"What's strange about that? Don't computer systems do that regularly?" Joshua inquired.

"Not this type of backup. This is the type of backup that only happens if the system might be in danger," Gavin explained.

"In danger of what?" Joshua posed.

"The exact thing we saw outside," Alex said, standing up and crossing his arms.

"What do you mean by that? Are you saying we got attacked?" Joshua asked.

"Makes sense. Remember the rising tensions before we left and the nuclear symbol Nora found? Not to mention the radioactive fog we encountered leaving the Cryo-chamber ruins. It all points to one thing," Gavin summarized while leaning over the terminal.

"Nuclear annihilation," Alex stated, the word hanging in the air like a thousand pounds of dead weight.

Slowly Alex could feel the pit in his stomach begin to widen as it started to encompass his midsection and snake like poison to his throat. Everyone had died his mother, his sister, old friends and acquaintances. All gone in a matter of moments, people he had left to prosper cut down without thought by the cruelty of war. No, he couldn't think like that those were thoughts for another time and another place he was the Pathfinder he had a job to do even if he was only making it up on the spot. His team needed him, So with a grunt of mental exertion he cut the head off the poisonous snake flowing through his blood and covered the pit of despair with stone.

"No wonder people don't remember the past. We killed ourselves and erased all of our achievements," Gavin said wearily. "The survivors must have started over completely."

"It might also explain the magic. Who knows what a thousand years of radiation damage could have done?" Alex theorized while rubbing his chin.

"Even make magic?" Joshua asked incredulously.

"More like grant access to a hidden form of energy some people can tap into," Gavin theorized with a bit of reassurance to his own understanding of the world.

"As great as that is, we still don't have an answer. What happened to the colony ship?" Alex restated.

As he said that, a notification appeared on the screen in front of them. Lines of running text filled the white notification box like a typewriter with super speed. From the first few lines, Alex could tell the system was performing maintenance or repair. He couldn't tell what commanded this maintenance, but it seemed to be very important, as the system appeared to divert a massive amount of resources to it.

"Gavin, what is it working on?" Alex asked, but the notification disappeared almost as quickly as that question left Alex's lips. A new notification replaced it and read, "Maintenance finished. Colony ship ready for departure."

"Well, that answers my question," Alex stated while trying to work through the waves of shock hitting him. "Any idea where it might be?"

"It will take a minute to figure that out," Gavin said,

tapping at the keys.

To everyone's surprise, a trumpeting sound rang through the halls outside the vault's door. Rylan had already unsheathed his sword. Suddenly, a creature bolted from the darkness and tackled Rylan to the ground, trying to rip him apart with its long claws and razor-sharp teeth. In the grapple, Rylan's sword slide to the other side of the room. With a quick burst of speed, Rylan grabbed the sword as it hit the wall and rammed it deep into the creature's neck with a sickening squelch. The beast batted at him with the side of its head, knocking him to his butt before scrambling out of the vault, leaving behind a trail of blood.

"Necrophages," Rylan said as Alex scrambled to get back to his feet. "There will be more of them soon, no doubt."

"And now we're defenseless," Alex mumbled to himself. "Gavin, how long do you need to get that info?"

"A few minutes at best. The system is straining off the backup as it is, and if I push it any harder, we'll lose the system and the data," Gavin answered, hunched over the computer terminal.

"Damn it! All right, ready up. We'll have to leave quickly and make a run for it," Alex ordered as he headed to the vault door.

"Wait, there might be another way," Gavin said as he stood up from the terminal and began searching the back of the room. "The data vault acted as a time capsule should anything ever happen to the company. If the rest of the vault is in the same condition, there should be some working equipment we can use."

Gavin led the group to the back of the room. There was a lot more to this room than a bunch of hard drives and computer towers. A plexiglass door led to a small corridor connecting another room. Pushing the door to the side, Alex could see that, at one point, it had been pressurized. However, it appeared to have fallen apart over the years, indicating the seal must have broken at some point. Inside the smaller room were rows of compartments, each held in place by a security lock.

"All right. New plan. Pick a safe and find something we can use," Alex ordered, running to the nearest compartment and pulling on the handle. "Anyone have a hammer?"

Luckily, the compartments were labeled. This made the search a lot easier. They rushed to the three compartments labeled "weapons".

"Here, use this," Rylan said, handing Alex a knife.

"Thanks," Alex replied as he rammed the knife's blade into the compartment and broke the lock.

Alex handed the knife back to Rylan and pulled the locked drawer out of its compartment, revealing a near-pristine heavy machine gun. This was the Mk1 Avenger, an assault rifle made in the style of a small compact mini-gun, with an internal canister clip and five rotating barrels. This weapon spewed bullets, but with the maneuverability of a regular assault rifle.

Pulling the weapon from its case, Alex looked over to Joshua and tossed it to him before removing the padding, revealing the weapon underneath, which looked like a miniaturized assault cannon mixed with a rifle. He recognized this as the PC-17, a really expensive, weaponized laser pointer that could cut through human flesh in one brief burst of energy. Alex never really enjoyed using them. They acted more like a high-powered sniper rifle without a scope, and the time to fire another shot was shit. Pulling the gun from the drawer, he turned to hand it to Gavin, only to find him examining something else he pulled from another opened compartment.

"Hey, Buddy! What you got there?"

"It's a working B.C.I. I didn't think these things were finished yet," Gavin exclaimed, holding up what looked like a pressurized syringe with a red button.

"What's a B.C.I.?" Alex asked as Gavin as they exchanged weapons.

"It stands for Bio Command Interface. It's the military version of a Holo-chip," Gavin explained in excitement. "Before we left, it was scheduled to be in R&D for a downgrade, since the testers died from brain hemorrhaging."

"Defective?" Alex asked.

"No, too powerful," Gavin answered.

As Gavin finished the sentence, a faint howl sounded behind them.

"How do I use it?" Alex asked, examining the device in a frenzy.

"It's an injection that goes inside the eye," Gavin answered, "but it's dangerous without proper medical equipment."

Another howl responded, closer this time.

"They're getting closer," Rylan stated, pulling another knife from a sheath.

"Is it worth it?" Alex asked, looking into the injector side of the device. "Maybe…I don't know," Gavin stumbled as he readied the laser weapon.

Another howl echoed into the room, this time very close. They had little time, and if this B.C.I. was powerful enough that it had to be downgraded, it sounded just like the edge they needed.

Just then, almost as if in slow motion, Alex heard Nora, who had been quiet up to this moment, scream as a bulky shape slammed into the room, slashing at Joshua. The force of the impact knocked him back into the wall. Gavin readied a shot and fired into the creature's side, only for it to turn toward him with a gaping hole in its chest, ready to pounce. Rylan tried to hold off the creature pushing through the entrance while Nora grabbed at her knife, flinging it through the doorway at another beast outside of his line of sight. A long arm lashed out, knocking Rylan to the floor and letting the creature he had been wrestling with inside.

"This is gonna suck," Alex exclaimed as he put the injector of the syringe into his right eye and pushed the button.

Chapter 14

The first beast ran through the door, knocking Nora to the ground, her knife falling from her hand. She was fairly certain she was dead as the creature leaped at her. But suddenly, a beam of some type of magic pierced through its side. Looking toward the source, Gavin held an unknown device, still pointing it in the creature's direction. A thin line of smoke wafted off the slits in its side. In another part of the room, Alex himself took the thing in his hand and rammed it into his right eye.

He began convulsing as if struck by a lightning spell. He fell limp for a few seconds, then stood up. Nora wanted to run over and help, but Alex immediately stood to attention, but in a way that seemed alien to her.

"Well, this is new," Alex said as another undead leaped at him.

Surely, Alex was about to be tackled and killed, but the creature didn't make it to his neck. Instead, it hung above the floor, struggling at arm's length from Alex.

"Okay, let's go," Alex said, as he punched the beast down to the ground and stomped its head in.

Grabbing her knife, Nora stabbed the side of an approaching monster after drawing its attention. At that instant, she focused on staying still and concentrating on her thoughts. From her fingers, she launched her magic "Firebolt", an orb of fire that flew straight at the monster's face. The beast howled in pain in response to its nowseared flesh and lunged at her in retaliation, only to fall to pieces as something, followed by a loud sound, ripped through it.

In the deafening noise's direction, Alex held a device similar to the one he had given Gavin, except this one had a different shape. Smoke emanated from a tiny port in the front. She didn't have time to question him about its nature. Alex turned the end of the device toward the doorway. Another deafening sound from the weapon soon followed.

In the doorway, the limp body of a necrophage lay dying on the floor. Rylan, the first to be attacked, tugged at his ears. It was then she noticed her own ears felt as if someone had stuffed them with cotton. All the surrounding noises seemed muted.

"Joshua, get on that door, lay down some cover fire!" Alex ordered, but Nora could barely hear him.

"Why is my hearing like this?" Nora asked as she tried to get back up.

"It's called tinnitus. It'll suck for a bit, but you'll be fine," Gavin said. Nora could barely hear what Gavin said.

Soon, a familiar sound rang through the air as Joshua pointed the weapon Alex had thrown him out the door. She needed a minute for her ears to recover from the deafening noise. So, with a brief unconscious thought, she cast "Barrier" on the open door. An enormous wall of multicolored energy immediately rose in place of where the door had been, blocking any more monsters from entering, for now.

"What the hell is this?" Joshua exclaimed.

"It's a barrier spell used to create a defensive line in battle," Rylan explained as he ran toward Nora. "It could last from a couple of minutes to an hour, depending on the strength of the caster."

"Okay then, here's the plan. Joshua and I will hold off the monsters for as long as we can. Gavin, get those files from the terminal and then rendezvous with us outside," Alex said as he pulled something from the device and then reconnected it. "Rylan, you and Nora follow close behind me and Joshua, and we'll escort you out of here. Understood?"

"Understood!" Rylan replied as he pulled something out of a side pouch and spread it around her ears. Almost instantly, the ringing in her ears was gone and the sensation she realized was dizziness had left as well.

"Feeling better?" Rylan asked her.

"Yeah, that's a lot better," Nora answered, pushing herself up from the floor.

"Good, we have to go now," Rylan said, grabbing her by her arm and pulling her toward the door.

"What was that?" she asked as she tripped over on of the bodies on the ground.

"Bear's Paw it strengthens the body and removes most temporary ailments," he answered as he steadied her.

"I've never heard of it, is it a medicine from the kingdom of Forstye," she asked.

"Yeah, it does," he said as more shots rang out from

past the doorway.

"Is there anything I can do to help?" Nora asked as Rylan grabbed her hand and dragged her forward.

"Stay behind me and stick to defensive magic," Rylan said, running through the door after Alex and Joshua.

Following closely, Nora readied another healing spell in her left hand while using her right to hold on to the edge of the wall. Her three companions weaved through the darkness of the corridors like they had taken a potion of dark vision. Using her magic as a source of light, she barely kept up with them, jumping over debris just as they appeared in her field of view.

It wasn't long before they reached the surface again, only this time, as they approached the exit of the stairwell, the snarls of a necro met them, pouncing at them. Concentrating her magic into a shield spell, Nora prepared to block the attack, only to see the creature's head explode into pieces as a beam of red light shot from Joshua's weapon ripped through it. She barely had enough time to register the attack before another burst of light ripped through a second necro hidden behind its comrade.

"I am finished being knocked on my ass by you monster fuck heads," Joshua exclaimed as he unleashed another beam of light through the stairwell's exit.

"Maybe they just want a piece of your booty," Alex retorted as he ran through the doorway Joshua just fired his weapon through.

"I seriously doubt I'm their type!" Joshua laughed as he followed Alex through the doorway.

Running after them, Nora and Rylan exited the building, only to be greeted by the gloomy, overcast sky of the ruins. In front of her, Alex fired his weapon in short, controlled bursts, killing each of the monsters before they could reach them while Joshua launched more devastating beams of light at the creatures farther away.

The entire scene unfolded like something out of fantasy for Nora. Normally, a squad of five King's-Glaive would have trouble taking down a horde of the six Necros, yet here, standing before her, stood two men holding off more than their fair share. She was so caught up in this scene that it completely surprised her when Rylan pushed her to the ground.

Looking back, Nora realized he had pushed her out of the way of a pouncing Necro with a blade stuck in its head. He rolled over onto the beast's back and sliced its head in two. In close view, Nora realized the sword in Rylan's hand was the sword that he lost to the first creatures they encountered earlier. With his weapon in hand, a fire reignited in his eyes and he jumped out into the ensuing fight, slashing at any creatures that dared to get close to them.

Running into the fray, Nora pooled magic in her hands and used it to craft a shield, which she cast upon Rylan just as a monster tried to jump on him from behind. This sent the creature flailing as it slammed into an emerald green wall. She then turned her attention over to the Precursors and noticed that some monsters broke through their line of fire and began closing in on them.

Readying a shield spell, Nora prepared to cast it upon the duo until she saw Alex sidestep the attack, kill the monster as it missed, and then pirouette around two more of the monster attacks before killing them in an instant. She watched as his movements became very fluid, mov-ing around the monsters like a professional dancer, almost in the same way and style that Rylan fought. Joshua, on the other hand, stood like a sentinel, making only the slightest movements before firing a beam of light that effectively killed each of his targets.

"Guys, I stripped the hard drive. We need to go now!" Gavin shouted from inside.

"You heard him. Guys, group up and run for the storm wall," Alex yelled as he dealt with five monsters at once.

Nora thought that running into the storm wall would be just as suicidal as staying here and fighting the necrophages, but Rylan interrupted her thoughts by grabbing her arm and pulling her away from the battle. They ducked beneath a leaping monster as it crashed into the ground beside them, where Rylan swiftly removed its head with a clean chop before leading her down an alley toward the shortest way to the storm wall.

The Precursors had wandered off, and Rylan was leading her in a mad dash down the crumbling alleyways and streets. She wondered if she and Rylan had left them behind when she heard their weapons discharging nearby, followed by a snide remark from Joshua about Gavin being too slow.

Nora wondered if this was normal for warriors to do, then she remembered all the times she heard other fighters jest and joke during their training exercises. She decided she would have to talk to them about it later, but she couldn't help but notice how super effective they still were. She was still pondering this when a body came hurtling out of nowhere and smashed into the wall to her left in a splatter of blood. It didn't take long for it to get up and begin chasing after them.

She picked up her pace as best she could and jumped over the pile of rubble in front of her, leaping directly into the wall on the other side and sliding down into the street below with Rylan. Hitting the ground with her feet, she clutched Rylan's arm tighter as something went flying over them and through the crumbling wall they just slid down.

One lone necrophage standing on two limbs glared menacingly at them as she looked over her shoulder. It then sucked in its midsection and screamed a blood-curtailing howl. In response, dozens of shadows accumulated inside and around the buildings behind her before erupting into a mass of Necrophages that chased after them.

A volley of sound raced over her head, causing her to duck, followed by a reassuring grip around her arm that yanked her forward and onto something metallic. Looking up, it appeared to be a sled of some kind. Two gigantic monsters held together by a large piece of metal yanked them forward while viscously snapping at each other's heads. The monsters she now faced looked rather leathery, with canine legs bursting to the brim with muscle, and a thin pig-like tail tucked between their legs.

"You have grey lurkers?" Nora heard Rylan yell at someone behind her. "Where the fuck did you find grey lurkers?"

"I don't know. Joshua found them in a shed somewhere. Is it a problem?" Alex replied.

Slowly, Nora's mind raced, trying to remember anything about grey lurkers. It sounded so familiar for some reason, but also very foreign.

"Where's the mother?" Rylan asked in a desperate tone, trying to get the urgency of the situation across to Alex.

That triggered her memory. She remembered where she had heard of them; she read about them in a passage from a monster tome recently. *Grey lurkers were loyal watchdogs and servants, protecting any person they considered their master. However, surviving an encounter with one is extremely rare. They are typically guarded over their by mother who…*

She didn't let that thought finish. She gained the answer to Rylan's fear. An enormous mass of dust and dirt exploded right next to them and took shape, becoming a single hulking mass of grey, leathery skin and boar-like tusks.

"Great! Mama is pissed," Rylan said as he ran past Nora's spot on the sled and began shouting at the top of his lungs at the racing lurkers to go faster.

"Guys, go faster!" Nora heard Alex yell, which prompted her to look in the direction he was shouting. Joshua and Gavin rode on top of the creatures, nudging them to go faster like one would a horse.

Alex's weapon rang out again, which prompted her to turn her attention back toward the grey lurker chasing them. Compared to the size of the ones pulling them along, this one was massive and stood at least 40 feet tall. Yet, despite its size, Alex simply continued to fire his weapon at it. Wondering why Alex kept firing at it, Nora felt a hand grab her and hold her down against the sled. As she hit the sled, a pair of claws sliced through the air in front of her face before weapon fire ripped apart it.

"Everybody, hold on!" Gavin shouted.

The sled jerked upward as the terrain inclined. She was about to ask how much farther to the storm wall, when the wind suddenly rushed in around the sled, blocking out the sound of her voice and sucking the air from her lungs. Above her, swirling clouds and large masses of dirt and rock flew about violently. She felt an updraft grab her, trying to rip her from the sled.

As it lifted her upward, she felt a hand latch onto her torso and pull her back down, anchoring her there. Nora turned, expecting to see Rylan once again, acting as her savior, only to find that he was holding on to the side of the makeshift sled with both hands. She traced the arm of her hero back to Alex, who appeared to have thrown himself onto her, keeping her safe. A bright flash of light jutted into the ground behind them, blowing more rock and debris into the air, followed by another one behind them and another one to their side, each flash accompanied by an ear-splitting crash of sound.

Lightning. Where had the lightning come from? When we entered, we didn't have to deal with this, Nora thought as another crash resounded somewhere in front of them. An unknown impact threw the sled to its side, sending her into the air once more. Looking for the source of the disturbance, she saw a giant paw swipe the air above the sled; the Mother Grey Lurker now followed them.

However, this fear soon revealed itself moot as a lightning bolt struck the massive beast, blowing off a part of its head as the wind picked up and lifted it up into the air. Nora almost felt relieved as their sled ascended slowly, lifting until they were a couple of feet in the air.

Gradually, the view from the bottom of the sled changed. The air cleared, accompanied by a dark, stormy cloud cover. They were outside of the perpetual hurricane, but she became terrified at the idea of falling. The sled that held her plummeted to the ground, landing on its side and lodging itself in the dirt.

"Are we dead yet?" Nora heard Rylan ask as he let go of his spot.

"All in favor of setting up camp, say aye," Alex said.

"Aye!" everyone responded.

***

Nora sat, tending to a small fire she had started, watching Gavin trying to feed the only surviving grey lurker. Off to the left of her vision, Nora could see Rylan and Alex returning to camp after their search for supplies. Slowly, she let her vision drop back to the fire as she stirred the hot embers with a long stick; the heat playing a string of mirages across her eyes.

She let her thoughts drift wildly. Images of the day's events played through her head, which stirred up more questions than answers for her. Nora thought she knew most of the Precursors' history—they ascended beyond humans, said to return and bring prosperity, and they represented the pinnacle of power—yet she stood among them now, no more the gods of white and gold robes than any other person. How could she have been so wrong in her understanding of them? Was everything written about their greatness a lie?

Sliding her hand into her bag, Nora pulled forth the old leather-bound book she read to the city children what felt like ages ago. She opened it and noticed that one of the pages had ripped its side, leaving a jagged edge to the once well-kept article. She turned it to the page she had last left off with the children. Its words seemed far away from the reality that surrounded her. Surely, it couldn't be possible that these Precursors were merely what they seemed. No doubt they hid their true nature so as not to be so overbearing while in our presence.

"Hey, what do you have there?"

Looking up from the book in her hands, Nora noticed Joshua sitting across the fire from her.

"Oh, it's nothing really. Just a journal from your time," Nora said, looking back down at the aged cover. "I found it well preserved in some ruins a while ago."

"Really, that's a stroke of good luck right there, especially with it being like over a thousand years old. I'm surprised it hasn't turned to dust yet," Joshua said. "How did you keep it in such a fine condition?"

"Oh, I submerged it in a potion of Gentle Repose. It's normally used in the slowing of flesh deterioration by necromancers, but when applied to paper and leather, it keeps it from falling apart," Nora explained while holding out the book and showing him the pages.

"Wait! Necromancy is a thing?" Joshua asked in a way that told her he found that idea troubling.

"Only to an extent…kingdom law forbids true necromancy," Nora answered as quickly as she could, afraid that they perceived it as a bad thing.

"Oh okay, you have to understand, in my time, we didn't have magic. The most magical thing was love, and even that had its limit," Joshua said as Nora watched him mess with a speck of dirt on the ground.

"That can't be true. Our texts spoke of you being of great power, shadowing anything we could hope to create," Nora argued, holding the book close to her chest. "Your sciences, literature, music, and weapons are said to be far greater than anything we could imagine."

"Nora, I'm sorry to say this, but that's simply not true. People from my time had many innovations, but they were truly no different from you now," Joshua began. "Power doesn't equal greatness, just as objects don't equal happiness or knowledge equals wisdom. Your people probably have achieved greatness akin to ours and have done so in a way that we could never follow. My time—if I've learned anything today—is like the great Ozymandias now, doomed to boast of our wonders to a world that has long passed us by."

"Then what's the point of all this?" Nora asked as Joshua's words broke through her wall. This was her truth. "Surely, you guys didn't just enter a forgotten city, risking your lives for nothing."

"The point is, we need to know where we stand, Nora," Joshua answered after a deep inhale of breath. "Do we abandon who we were, or is there something worth salvaging? The other two are clinging to hope because, without it, they have nothing."

"And not you?" Nora asked, looking into Joshua's eyes.

"It would be miraculous if their hope proved true, but after what I've seen today, I'm not holding out hope. The only path I see now is to leave the past buried," Joshua finished with a thoughtful sigh.

"And if their hope proves true?" Nora asked.

"Then maybe we can save something," Joshua answered.

Their discussion ended. They both sat there, silently, and stared into the fire—the silence broke only moments later by a high-pitched chime. Looking up from the hazy illusions of the fire, Nora followed the sound over to Gavin, who displayed a strange light device from his arm. He let out a shriek of delight and ran over to the fire, laughing.

"Guys! Guys! I did it! Haha."

"Did what, Gavin?" Alex asked, assaulted by the jumping, happy form of his friend.

"I found the Colony ship! I found it!" Gavin exclaimed. "It didn't make any sense. Why did they leave us behind? Pathfinder teams are priority number one. Even in the event of a catastrophe, Pathfinders are designated V.I.P. and instantly deployed to the main ship. If that were the case, then they would have moved us."

"So, what?" Joshua asked while standing up.

"We weren't moved, so I ran a simulation on if the colony ship had orbited over the course of a thousand years and tracked it to its estimated position."

"And?"

"It never left. It's still here. We never got left behind!"

"So wait, the ship is still in orbit?" Alex asked, his body tense with excitement.

"No. Actually, due to the slingshot maneuver, which we used to start the initial propulsion of the colony ships, the decay of the ship's orbit would force it to land on the planet. After the first few hundred years, it would fall back to earth and the emergency landing equipment would engage," Gavin explained hysterically.

"Gavin, please calm down and explain slowly. Where did the ship land?" Joshua asked, grabbing Gavin's shoulders.

"According to my scanner, it landed over there," Gavin said after taking a deep breath and pointing to the forest to their southwest.

"That's impossible," Nora interjected, looking at the forest. "That's the Twilight Forest. Nothing is in there except monsters and darkness, not to mention it's nearly impossible to traverse without a guide! Right, Rylan?"

"Right. We had a run-in with some of its inhabitants when we came to find you," Rylan responded.

"But there are guides?" Alex asked, as a plan formed in his head.

"Yeah, one joined us shortly after our encounter. He helped get your teammate back to our kingdom," Rylan answered.

"So, we head back to your kingdom and ask this guy to help search for our ship. No big deal," Alex said as he calculated in his head how long the detour would take.

"Might also want to bring a healer, too; you were in pretty terrible shape when we found you," Nora replied.

"Gavin, how long could the Cryo-containment system of the ships operate?" Alex asked as a thought jumped to the front of his mind.

"Near indefinitely—with constant maintenance from the yearly engineering crew and a constant power supply. Why?" Gavin answered.

"Gavin, I think it's safe to assume the ship hasn't had an engineering crew in a long while," Alex said as he felt excited optimism change into pure dread.

"How long would the passengers have to survive?" Alex asked as he checked the B.C.I. for a watch.

"Assuming that all systems are fully functional, nothing has happened to the generator, the life support system is still operational, and age hasn't damaged the Cryo-pods since it crashed, they should have about five days," Gavin replied, looking up from the quick calculations he just performed on his Holo-chip.

"Five days to survive after they crashed?" Joshua asked.

"No, we have five days to find them before the colonist's Cryo-pods give out," Gavin responded, as Alex found an alarm clock feature on his device and set the time to a minute less than five days.

"So we find the ship and save them, we have plenty of time to get there,"

"Not from these coordinates," Joshua interjected, "based on the density of the forest and how long it took us to get to our current position it would take us at best ten."

"Is there any way to connect to the ship from here?" Alex asked.

"If we had a wireless router and a signal booster I could try to reduce the strain of the ships nonfunctional systems on the power core but that's a big if and it would only give us a couple hours," Gavin replied.

"We could go back into the ruins and see what we can find?" Joshua suggested.

"Oh sure, I always wanted to know what it felt like to be a monster buffet," Gavin sarcastically answered, "Besides by the time we find what we need if it's still operational we still won't have enough time to get to the ship."

Silently Alex ran the scenario through his head while biting what remained of his thumb nail. As his friends argued a grunting cry bellowed out behind him which finally gave him the solution they needed.

"Joshua is the sled still intact?" Alex asked.

"Yeah for the most part, I mean we'd have to pry it from the ground but its not unusable," joshua reported.

"Would we be able to make it there in time if we use the creature," Alex suggested with a hand gesture to their remaining beast.

"Thing's about as fast a horse maybe a bit faster and it was able to carry us without any problem," Gavin calculated, "we'd probably reach it with hours to spare if we could."

"Problem is the forest, if the trees are too close together we can get stuck," Joshua injected.

"Can you find us a path that might work," Alex asked.

"Without a map of the area or any knowledge of the forest it would take just as long to chart a course," Joshua answered.

"Unless there's someone who already knows the area. Alright, here's what we'll do," Alex said, looking over his team. "Gavin, I want you to upload those coordinates to our Holo-chips and do whatever prep you need for a mass Cryo-wake sequence. Joshua, you're on point. I need you to find us a direct route to the ship. Call Daniel and ask him to put you in contact with that guide he can help you plot a course through the forest. Meanwhile I'll ready the creature and reattach the sled. Be ready to leave in 30 minutes."

Having given orders to his team, Alex turned his attention to Rylan and Nora, who were still standing patiently. He honestly didn't know what to do with them; they had helped so much already and to ask anything else of them seemed unfair. However, thinking back on what they had said, it would be helpful if they joined them.

"I can't ask you to join us, especially after all that's happened, but if you wish to join us, we could use your help," Alex said to them after a couple of seconds of silence.

"We've come this far. Might as well stay for the end of this crazy ride," Rylan answered, smiling.

"Of course. Besides, precursor or not, people need our help. We can't just abandon them," Nora added while stuffing a brown book into her bag.

"All right then. If there's anything you can do to help us before we leave, please do so," Alex said, gesturing for them to fill in where they could.

Within the next hour, not only had they gained a quick map of the area established by Joshua and the ranger, but they had also gained the aid of the nearby kingdom of Somnium, who agreed to send healers and a guard contingent once the party cleared the area for entry. Removing the sled from the earth and attaching it to the remaining creature they set off into the forest at a brisk speed.

Upon entering the forest, Alex observed an instant change in the light and atmosphere; it was as if they had entered an entirely different world. In the corner of his eye, a display showing a reading of anomalous energies in the atmosphere popped up.

"Hey Gavin, I'm getting strange readings from the atmosphere here. You think it's because of the ship?" Alex asked as they passed a cluster of strange trees he had never seen before.

"That might explain the twilight effect. If the ship's asteroid impact field was even slightly functional, it might distort the lights' wavelength," Gavin answered.

"Is that a good thing for us or a bad thing?" Alex asked as they vaulted a fallen tree.

"Not sure, we'll probably learn more the closer we get," Gavin replied with his eyes steadily keeping track of the map.

"We might have our answer sooner," Joshua interjected, stopping the sled in it's tracks.

"What do you got?" Alex asked while surveying the area.

"Tracks on the ground, gait pattern is strange, but I think it might be humanoid," Joshua answered while directing their attention to a series of markings on the ground. "Whatever it is it's heading in the direction we're going."

"Any idea what this might be?" Alex asked, turning to Rylan.

"Might be the Blights. Never seen their tracks, though; they mostlysort of float off the ground," Rylan answered.

"Blights?"

"Strange plant-like beings that live in these woods. According to reports, they've been very active lately, kidnapping people and attacking villages."

"Is that unusual?"

"Very! They're known to be quite peaceful."

"Then we should be careful," Alex said, gesturing with his hand forhis team to proceed forward.

Chapter 15

Gazing upon the marvel before her, a vessel as tall as the trees protruded from the ground like a metallic hill. From what she was told, it barely constituted a fifth of the ship itself. Nora could feel the artificer in her blood yearning to explore its interior to find out what made it tick, but that would have to wait till later. Scores of Blights floated around the area in front of them, moving in and out of a hole in the ship, carrying materials and other items.

To her left sat Alex, aiming his weapon at the creatures in a crouching posture. Nora immediately realized she had learned about Alex's posture from the tales of the hunters when eyeing their prey.

"I count ten on my side," Joshua's voice silently sounded from the glowing orange light on Alex's wrist.

"I can't believe what I'm seeing. According to my scans, these creatures aren't organic, it's only the exterior. Underneath, the shell is actually a complex system of robotics," Gavin's voice chimed in over the device.

"I thought the robotic units were supposed to be simple drones," Alex whispered.

"They were. Last I heard, they're glorified can openers, not fully operational quasi-androids," Gavin chirped over the device.

Alex clicked his tongue as he pulled part of his weapon off and checked the inside before replacing it. "Okay, here's the plan. Josh, you and I are going to take them from the front and draw their attention away from the opening. Meanwhile, Gavin, I want you to slip inside and see what you can do for the colonists."

"What about us?" Rylan whispered as he slid onto his knees beside them.

"Rylan, I need you to clear a path for the inbound medical teams," Alex directed, pointing off in what Nora assumed was the direction of the castle. "Once that's done, make your way back to me and Josh."

"Got it," Rylan answered as he darted into the forest undergrowth.

"As for you, Nora, I need you to go in with Gavin and provide support. We don't know what the interior looks like or how bad of a shape the colonists are in. So, be ready for anything," Alex said, his eyes locking with Nora for a moment. Then he dashed into the undergrowth and down toward an advantageous spot.

Nora watched the Blights move in their floaty way from the hole in the vessel to the woods. In response, she heard the Precursors' weapons unleashing deadly bolts upon the enemies.

Taking the opportunity, Nora ran toward the hole in the vessel, meeting up with Gavin and swiftly ducking inside. Darkness greeted her gaze, but Gavin's wrist quickly stripped it away with a beam of light, illuminating a metallic corridor overgrown with plant life.

"Structural integrity doesn't seem to have decayed much over the years, but I doubt the ship remained intact upon impact with the planet. That helps us, though. If the ship is mostly intact, then we should have no trouble getting to the Cryo-controls," Gavin said as he began jogging down a hall.

"I'm assuming that these Cryo-controls will help us save everyone on board," Nora inquired while chasing after him.

"Yes, we can use them to activate wake-up protocol, which will pull everyone from Cryo," Gavin answered as they turned a corner, heading into an even darker corridor.

As Nora ran down the corridors of the station, she noticed glass panels lining areas near doors and hallways in the dim glow of Gavin's light. Quietly, she wondered how such architecture and innovation failed to intrigue or gain even a small bit of interest from her companion. Had she the time, she knew she could spend hours examining the intricacies of each of the doors.

Turning a corner, Nora found a round door with a circular indentation in the middle, blocking their way.

"What is this?" Nora asked as she saw Gavin rush to the indentation and press his thumb against it.

"Cryo-chamber is behind this door," Gavin said as he checked the indentation panels. "Normally, the door should open once I hit the button, activating the emergency release. Unfortunately, it doesn't look like we've got any power left in the system, so I'll have to do it manually."

"Is there a way to get power to the door?" Nora asked, scanning the area for something that could help.

"The main generators are supposed to provide backup power in case this ever happens," Gavin explained as he messed with the wires of the door. "Bet you ten bucks that those robots did this. They probably tampered with the electrical output to keep the Cryo-chamber from running."

"Is there anything we can do?"

"Not here, there isn't." With a flick of his wrist, Gavin activated the strange light device. "Alex, we've got a problem. We're locked out of the Cryo-chamber and I can't open the doors."

"Any suggestions?" Alex responded over the device.

"We need to redirect secondary power to the auxiliary systems of the ships, then I can begin the thawing process," Gavin said as they ran down another hallway.

"Let's do that then," Alex responded.

Soon, Gavin and Nora found themselves in what looked like small, round rooms.

"Already on it," Gavin answered as he ran into one of the small rooms. "What are these?" Nora asked, getting in beside him.

"Transit cars. They run the length of the ship and connect to each main hub area. Unfortunately, with the power out, we'll have to run along their tunnels to the next section." Gavin pulled up a hatch on the floor and slid into it.

Nora followed suit and found herself underneath the transit car. After crawling forward a bit, she found herself in a large, cavernous tunnel.

Gavin led the way with the light from his wrist and they raced down the tunnel. As they ran, Nora saw other openings along the way, each with a small, detailed inlay that described what she guessed was the function of each area.

Nora was busy in her own mind when she suddenly ran into Gavin, who quickly caught her in his arms and put a hand over her mouth. Confused, Nora protested, demanding why he was doing this. Then she saw it.

Chapter 16

Blights! Lots of them laying prone on the ground in heaps, small strings connecting from their heads to a panel on the ground, their yellow eyes closed. Slowly, Nora regained herself. Gavin held a finger up to his mouth and held up three fingers, followed by a crude zero with a cupped hand. There were thirty of them, more than they could hope to fight by themselves, especially with such limited weapons. Even Nora's magic wouldn't be enough to change the odds.

Catching slight movement out of the corner of her peripheral vision, Gavin held out a hand to her and pointed to the platform to the right of the hostile mass. Looking for a sign, Nora could barely make out a broken plaque of metal engraved with the words "power core". Tiptoeing, she followed Gavin as he stepped over limp tendrils and limbs, slowly making his way to the platform.

Following in his steps, the sight of the limbs evoked unpleasant feelings from Nora's core as she walked over them. Looking closely at them, Nora could tell they were

a mishmash of different materials. Some pieces had been supplemented from tree bark and stones. Plants, moss, and vines helped hold together various parts,
wrapping around entire sections.

As she examined the creatures, a tentacle came snaking out in front of her feet, tripping her as she attempted to step over another one of the creatures. She hit the ground with a loud clanging sound that echoed throughout the tunnel. For five seconds, Nora could swear everything held its breath as she laid prone and still on the floor. Her senses cranked themselves to the max in self-defense. Looking up at Gavin, urgency washed his face in a second, and with a quick motion, he pulled her up to her feet just as a sharp clang echoed next to her leg.

Time seemed to slow down and then jarringly sped up, as the sound of several Blights snapped and whirred behind her in an aching cacophony. Fear suddenly engulfed her. She felt her legs surge forth with energy as she sprinted with Gavin onto the platform. Looking over her shoulder, Gavin was sprinting along the hall with a group of Blights chasing closely behind them both.

Never had she felt this kind of fear, except for when she was young and the idea of a monster in her closet would force her to sprint to her parent's bed in the middle of the night. However, while the threat in her childhood was imaginary, this one was all too real, a bad dream scenario she had locked away in the back of her mind as a pure anxiety-driven fantasy.

Flying through the halls, Nora barely had time to exclaim when Gavin grabbed her arm and chucked her through a nearby door. How Gavin's thin frame could muster such strength, Nora could not fathom, but she was happy he could. Suddenly, a three-clawed tendril snapped right where she had just stood. Crouching, Gavin let loose a burst of fire from his weapon before jumping inside and shutting the door.

Looking around their new surroundings, Nora could tell they had reached the control room. Her previous forays in similar precursor buildings informed her that this might be where they could turn the power back on. The control hub was a singular glass room encased in a metal cage with a row of computer terminals facing out toward a giant room filled with a gigantic machine she could only describe as a huge cylindrical pillar encased in large pipes.

As they stood up, a long screech tore through the air behind them. Similar sounds emanated from the other side of the door. Tossing Nora his weapon, Gavin ran past her to the computer terminal. With a flick of his wrist across the screens, he turned on the array.

"That door won't hold them for long," Gavin stated, tapping on an assortment of buttons.

"How long do you need?" Nora asked as another sharp screech rang out behind them.

"Depends. If they didn't fuck up the system, then it could be a couple."

"And if they did?"

"39 minutes to an hour…" Gavin scanned the outputs that flashed across the monitors.

A loud clang rang out behind them, followed by the sound of air and gears squealing under external pressure. The doors were being pried open from the outside. Thin rays of red light seeped through cracks where the door had already given way. Grabbing the rifle from Nora's hands, Gavin took aim down the crack and sent a couple of bursts through to the other side, before handing it back to her and resuming his display of finesse and expertise. His hands swept across the controls in a frantic symphony of movement. However, this only delayed the intrusion, as once more, the squealing sound of pressure against the door's locking mechanism returned.

"Stupid robots," Gavin muttered under his breath. "Unfortunately for you, I now have control."

Instantly, the large cylinder outside the control window turned slowly, its sections flaring in response to the starting sequence before it immediately halted.

"What the ass?" Gavin exclaimed as red warning lights lit up the monitors.

"What's wrong?" Nora asked.

"The battery system doesn't have enough power to re-initiate the starting sequence," Gavin replied as he brought up a schematic on the monitor. "However, if I drain power from one of the other systems, I can jumpstart the generator…ass!"

"No power?" Nora inquired, the sound of squealing reaching a crescendo behind her. "No, we have power. It's just in the one place we can't grab it from, which is the Cryo-chamber," Gavin answered as the sound of a loud snap rang out behind her, followed by the sound of screeching metal.

Gavin grabbed the rifle from Nora's hands again and wheeled around into a kneeling position, firing a volley of shots into the slowly opening doors. On the other side, the strange sounds of wailing and electricity responded, followed by frantic sweeping of metallic limbs flying through the crack, trying to slash at them.

At that instant, Nora cupped her hands together—

concentrating her magic—she launched four crystallized projectiles into the breach that exploded on impact, revealing the swirling mess of creatures outside the door, each reaching through the cracked door to grab them.

"We won't last long if we don't get that generator working," Gavin stated as he fired a couple more rounds into the breach.

"Can't we borrow the power from the Cryo-chamber?" Nora asked, her ears once again feeling as though someone had shoved cotton into them.

"Not unless we have someone inside immediately restart the system, otherwise we could lose the entire population in a matter of minutes," Gavin answered, firing again into the crack as a tentacle swept out through the hole and clipped him across the arm.

"How do we get someone inside if the door is locked?" Nora asked, pulling a dagger from her belt and slashing at a flailing limb.

"I can use the initial discharge to power the door and open it, but we'd need somebody to restart the Cryo-system immediately," Gavin explained as he fired a few more shots.

"What about the Blights?" Nora inquired as she fended off another tentacle.

"If I lower the electrical shielding around everywhere except the Cryo-chamber, the discharge should act like an EMP and short their systems," Gavin said, rushing to the control panel and quickly inputting several commands.

"Do you think Alex and Joshua could make it?" Nora asked, launching another round of magic missiles into the breach.

"They're going to have to." Gavin pulled up his glowing orange device.

Chapter 17

"We have a situation here," Alex heard over his communicator as he put a few rounds into an approaching robot.

After he had left Nora to begin the assault, he and Joshua held up in the cover of an uprooted boulder, laying down suppressive fire to keep the Blights at bay. While it wasn't the strongest tactical position, it provided suitable cover and allowed them to stay relatively safe from the slashing tendrils of the Blights.

"Talk to me," Alex responded as he let loose another volley of shots.

He had quickly grown to appreciate the B.C.I. as it displayed not only an aiming reticle across his vision but also an ammo counter for his weapon. Normally, he would just keep shooting till his weapon was empty and he would need to reload, or he would do the mental math to determine how many bullets he had left between each burst of fire. But with the ammo counter, he didn't need to worry about that and instead could use it to help plan his next move.

"We don't have enough juice in the system to start the generator and bring power back online to open the door," Gavin answered.

"Any ideas?" Alex asked as a robot lunged at the boulder.

"We need to divert the power from the Cryo-chamber to start the main generator, but we need to restart the Cryo-chamber immediately afterward, or we could lose everybody," Gavin explained as Alex unloaded into a Blight before it could attack.

"So, do it," Alex answered, as another set of tendrils snaked around the boulder and impaled themselves right next to his head.

"We can't. A horde of robots is trying to get in. They have us trapped in the generator's control room. We need you to do it," Gavin answered as Alex rolled out of the way of another set of tendrils slashing the air where he had just been.

"Fuck!" Alex cursed, shooting the owner of the tendrils. "Get the generator ready. We'll make a push for it. Josh!"

"Right," Joshua answered as he popped the safety on his grenade launcher and sent a round straight into the oncoming horde.

"Push!" Alex exclaimed, aiming down the barrel of his gun and charging into the opening while firing at any stragglers that were unfazed by the grenade.

In basic combat training, they taught you to never tunnel yourself into the world around you. A stray grenade, a ricochet bullet, a flanking enemy; all these things could spell death if you remained unaware. Now in the mess of these robots, Alex could feel his senses straining to catch all of it; the robots' tentacles, the fallen bodies beneath his feet, and the overwhelming sound of metallic screeching and whirring. The robot to his left had already recovered. Joshua released a spray of bullets, sending a lunging Blight to the ground with a controlled burst. It was overwhelming, but he could take it. He had to take it. Many lives counted on him. Since becoming Pathfinder, the idea of failure was never an option for him, and it would not be an option now.

In that moment, he slowed his breathing and focused on everything; his sight, his vision, his body, and mind all need to work as one. Noticing his gun ran out of ammo, Alex chucked the empty magazine and chambered his last cartridge right as he caught sight of another robot slashing at Joshua. He sent a quick burst into the robot before its tendrils could hit Joshua, sending it tumbling to the ground.

Stumbling forward, Alex crashed into the side of the jagged hole of the ship as another grenade whistled next to his ear and exploded inside the breached hull. Sucking breath into his lungs, Alex ran into the ship, pain coursing through his leg. As he entered, he glimpsed Joshua spraying down the approaching Blights, backing up to the entrance.

Running forward into the dark, the sight in his right eye clicked into night vision, the B.C.I. adapting to the environment for him. Suddenly, a robot fell from the roof and landed on top of Alex, pinning him to the wall with a clawed limb. The fingers of the claw dug through his clothes and into his flesh. Pointing the gun into the Blight's core, Alex fired a quick burst and knocked the dead body off him while ripping the claw free from his shoulder.

He was just in time to see another flying through the darkness at him, which he dispatched with another burst from his weapon, the body smacking into his chest with the power of a heavy metal softball. Tanking the hit, he pushed his body forward down the hall as his leg screamed in pain. The door to the Cryo-chamber was closed, thankfully. He just needed to get there and pray that Gavin had a way to take care of the robots. Rounding a corner, he saw the door to Cryo-bay in front of him, and the door's panel, laying discarded on the ground next to it.

"I'm here, Gavin. Hit the doors!" Alex ordered as he threw himself against the doorway.

"On it," Gavin responded.

As he waited for the doors to open, Alex felt himself lifted off the ground and flung into the wall opposite the doors. Looking up, a large Blight with razor-sharp appendages had snuck up on him and now loomed over him, blocking his way to the Cryo-chamber. He let off a few shots before the robot buried a spiked limb into his chest, lifting him farther up against the wall in the process. It barely flinched from the gunfire and instead sunk its spiked limb deeper into his chest.

Alex could feel himself blacking out, the edges of his vision clouding with dark spots. But then he heard the doors to the Cryo-chamber slide open as the surrounding ship hummed to life. The robot screamed in pain as electrical sparks shot from its body, its limbs flopping about with a life of their own. Using this wild movement to his advantage, Alex pushed himself from the wall, the robot's tendril still embedded inside his chest, and used the machine's erratic motion to fling him into the Cryo-room. He hit the metallic grating of the Cryo-room upon landing. The air left his lungs as a consequence of the impact. He felt the last of his consciousness fading.

"Start the Cryo-chamber now!" Gavin yelled, his

voice bringing Alex back to semi-reality.

Alex crawled forward to the control terminal and lifted his body onto the control board. His hands gradually going numb, he clumsily flicked the master power switches, and with staggering effort, forced his hand to hit the power button.

Instantly, the room lit up with cool blue lights, the sounds of the Cryopods internal mechanism starting up, and the quick release of pentup pressure from years of idle tubes resounded around him. Soon he felt a hand grab his shoulder. Looking up, Alex saw Joshua smiling, before unconsciousness took him and he felt his body slump against the cold Cryo-controls.

Chapter 18

Opening his eyes, Alex found himself in a very steril-
ized medical room. Thinking back to previous events, he
wondered if everything had been a fever dream. If he was
simply waking up on the colony ship. That was until he
saw the medical gauze and tape covering the injuries he
acquired during the fight.

"Good morning, Pathfinder."

Looking over to the owner of the voice, Alex saw
Barbra, their pilot, who spoke to him from a stool at the
side of the bed.

"Barbra," Alex said, trying to sit up, only to regret it
as pain coursed through his body in response.

"Whoa, calm down there, boss." Barbra rushed over
to help him lie back down. "You're not entirely fixed up
yet. Magic might be powerful, but it still has its limits."

"What happened?" Alex grunted, settling back into
the bed.

"Shortly after you booted up the Cryo-chamber,

Dan and Rylan showed up with the king's men, apparently Dan was able to levy some help from the kingdom on his own. They immediately brought you to the medical ward and started treating you. We began the thawing process and started pulling people from Cryo-sleep." Barbra pulled her stool closer and sat back down. "Since then, you've been recovering for the past three days."

"Is that all anything else," Alex joked.

"The captain has started relations with Somnium during which they will supply the ship and colonists with food, shelter, and medical aid while we begin the process of constructing a new city. Their king has even offered us the surrounding forest as a site to begin construction.

"Why is that,"

"Apparently the kingdom has had no use for it and had remained unused due to our robots," Barbra explained, "that and the soil isn't particularly good for farming or ranching so it's kinda dead weight to them."

"Dead soil can be fixed. What about the robots?" Alex asked, the pain shortly returning to his chest before subsiding.

"According to Joshua, the ones outside of the ship retreated into the forest before the EMP blast went off. The ones that stuck around were fried almost immediately," Barbra answered before entering into a coughing fit.

"What's wrong?" Alex asked as her fit subsided.

"My lungs haven't exactly returned to full strength since I woke up. The doctors think it's only temporary, but they don't know for sure."

"I'm so sorry. I should have…" Alex started, before Barbra placed a hand over his chest, stopping him.

"It's not your fault. We weren't expecting this, let

alone trained for it," Barbra rebutted, her stark green eyes holding him in their clutches. "Besides, it's not officially crippling yet. When it gets to that point, then I'll accept any and all apologies you have."

"Deal," Alex smiled.

In that moment, he heard a cough from behind Barbra and noticed one of the colony's militia officers standing at attention.

"At ease," Alex responded, realizing this was the first time he was being addressed as a high-ranking official.

"Sir, Captain Mercer would like to see you as soon as you've recovered," the officer said, his body still stiff.

"Understood. Tell the captain I'll see her as soon as I can," Alex answered with a nod.

"Yes sir." The officer walked out of the room the way he had come.

"That sounds like trouble," Alex mumbled once the officer left earshot.

"You'll get it figured out." Barbra gave Alex a quick pat on the leg. "Besides, you're the Pathfinder."

"Yeah," Alex said to himself as Barbra left him alone in the medical room.

***

It had been two days since the captain summoned Alex before he felt strong enough to leave the medical bay. During this time, Alex caught up with the rest of his crew and learned the remaining details of what happened after he passed out, though what Gavin had said worried him.

According to Gavin, while checking the ship's database to ensure all of the crucial files were intact, he ran across a large data transfer that took place minutes before the EMP went off. When he tried to check the file name or origin, he only found the name "Lazarus" before all traces of it disappeared from the system. When Alex asked if it was a code name for the space radio, Gavin answered that the radio had never been called that name through its entire conception and that it wasn't a part of any of those files.

Using a crutch the doctor gave him, Alex walked down the hall to the captain's office, his mind racing, trying to figure out the mystery behind the missing data. Had the robots taken it when they left or was it lost due to corruption? The answer seemed important to him, but he couldn't tell why. Maybe it was just his brain trying to make a puzzle out of nothing, he thought as he approached the door to the captain's office. Besides, he had more important things to deal with now.

Shelving his line of questioning to the back of his mind, Alex straightened himself up as best he could and knocked. The door opened with a satisfying swish, revealing an open reception area that led into a larger office. The captain sat behind a desk in the very back, looking over a terminal.

The captain was a middle-aged woman of African-American descent, Alex recalled, with a curious tribal-style tattoo in blue ink under her eyes. Her name was Arrana. At first, he wondered if it had any cultural significance but quickly dismissed the thought. The first time he met her was back before they went into hypersleep. He remembered that she wasn't exactly a fun person to be around. It was hard to get a read on her, though she gave off the impression that she didn't like him. For what reason? He didn't know. Stepping into the room, his crutch made a sharp clacking sound on the quasimetal surface of the floor, alerting the captain of his arrival. She spoke to him with a strong southern twang.

"Pathfinder, please have a seat," the captain said while motioning toward a cushioned chair, her attention still fixed on the terminal.

"Thank you, captain," Alex answered while easing himself into the chair. "What can I do for you?"

"Straight to business, I see," she replied, then with a wave of her wrist, shut down her terminal. "First off, let me thank you for your quick acting and performance in saving me and the rest of the ship. I also must thank you for beginning positive relations with the neighboring kingdom."

"You're welcome," Alex answered, unsure of where this was going.

"However, as useful as you and your team have been, we have no need for a pathfinder at this moment." She said, searching Alex's face for a reaction.

"I don't quite understand what you mean, Captain. Right now we need my skills more than ever," Alex argued while giving her his best poker face.

"How so?"

"This isn't the Earth we know anymore. For all intents and purposes, we're on a strange and dangerous planet with multiple factions and mysteries. The Pathfinder's job is to protect the colony and secure a safe haven, or somewhere for them to populate, while also dealing with first contact and exploration of unknown lands," Alex replied without lowering his poker face. "These are unknown and dangerous lands, Captain. Make no mistake about that."

"I see, while I can agree with you that things have

changed, I will argue that the kingdom is more than willing to help us understand our new home and help us settle a new colony," she argued, her eyes never leaving his face.

"For now," Alex answered, a tinge of anger welling in his stomach.

"However, from my time working with them, while they may know a lot, they don't know everything about their own world. In fact, parts of it are inaccessible to them. And if that isn't enough reason for me to resume my mission, there are more than likely several deposits around the world filled with experimental tech that could make this world very uninhabitable for everyone as my team can attest to from our experience in the lost city."

"I see. That being the case, I still do not see your job as anything we cannot remedy with a small team of scouts. Therefore, I've decided to disband your team," she answered, and for a second, Alex could see the hint of a grin cross her face. "Effective immediately."

"What will happen to my crew?" Alex asked, fuming.

"They will either take a role in the civilian workforce or may sign up for any open militia positions. As for you, since we've begun relations with the neighboring kingdom, we need a diplomatic envoy to conduct business with them and secure trade," she answered, her eyes almost cold and unfeeling. "Do you accept the position?"

"What if I don't?" Alex asked, the rebellious side of him hating that he was being forced into a position as a glorified peace offering.

"Then you may return to the civilian workforce," she replied, her voice dripping with venom. "Honestly, I don't care either way."

Gingerly, Alex tested his leg against the floor to see

if he could put his full weight on it; the response was a dull ache akin to a sprained ankle. He hated her; she was doing this on purpose for some ulterior motive. What it was, he couldn't fathom, though he suspected it had something to do with his position and not himself personally. Calmly, he closed his eyes and tried to quell his anger; he needed a clear head for this.

As an envoy with the kingdom, he could figure out a way to continue his mission, maybe even force her to listen to him if he could gain enough power. However, that would take time, a commodity that he felt they did not have. This world was, as he had stated before, not the same one they had left behind. To top it off, anything from their time was more than likely capable of being used against them or innocent civilians. Besides, he could already tell that even if he gained influence, she would simply find a way to use it in her favor.

"Thanks for the offer, but I think I'll pass," Alex answered, standing up from the chair on both legs. "I'm not a diplomat, and besides, I hate politics."

Alex turned around and walked to the door, the pain in his leg lessening with each step. Halfway through the door, he had the sudden urge to look back over his shoulder to see her expression, but shrugged it off. He didn't need to know. Besides, he could already tell she was smiling.

Exiting the ship via the hole in the side, Alex saw several people grouped outside, talking amongst themselves in the light of several campfires and a full moon. They had already completed some logging and cleared the foliage surrounding the ship, which opened the sky for stargazing.

"So, I just heard we got the boot," Alex heard Joshua say from behind him.

"Yeah." Alex turned around to see the rest of the team following him. "The captain seems to think we're useless now that we're not in space anymore."

"So, what are we going to do?" Gavin asked, a hint of concern garnishing his voice.

"Don't know. She said you can join the militia or become a civilian. Honestly, I think she might have some ulterior motive for all this," Alex answered.

"If that's true, she'll probably undermine anything we do," Dan replied, his face scowled up in frustration.

"More than likely, which is why I'm going to continue the mission without her," Alex answered, examining all their reactions. "This world is an untamed giant with mysteries and possibilities, some that could help us and some that can hurt us. We need to know about all of them and can't let them fall into the wrong hands. It's too dangerous and irresponsible."

"I agree," Barbra said, her face thoughtful for a moment. "I'll go with you,boss."

"Same here," Joshua piped up, sauntering over to him. "Already went through a horde of killer robots together."

"Well, we can't all go running off into the unknown. Who's going to monitor things here?" Gavin gestured back to the ship. "If the captain is up to something, somebody has to make sure things are safe here."

"I'll stay," Dan answered with a solemn nod. "I'll try to get a position that lets me move around with some freedom and keep an eye out. If anything fishy happens, I'll let you know."

"I should probably stay as well," Gavin replied after a minute. "They'll need me to help set up the subspace radio, and if not, I'll make sure they don't blow themselves up."

"Alright then. Tomorrow, we'll set off. Josh, see what you can smuggle from the armory for us. We'll need it. Barbra, look into getting a map and a vehicle for us. If you can't get the vehicle, see if you can find a frequency scanner. We'll use it to track down any other tech caches out there. We'll meet here at seven and head off east toward those floating islands," Alex commanded.

"You got it, boss," Barbra answered as she went back inside the ship.

"See you then," Joshua replied, following her.

"We'll go see if we can find anything else that might help." Gavin gestured to Dan to follow.

Standing in the open, staring after them as they entered the facility, Alex wondered if he was doing the right thing. But as he looked up to the sky, he felt a calm reassurance wash over him. The stars always seemed to do that for him, no matter his dilemma. Maybe he was just weird, but sometimes he could swear they talked to him.

"Hello," Alex heard a voice call out. Turning in the voice's direction, he saw Nora standing with a leather book in her hands.

"Hello," Alex replied with a slight wave.

"How are you doing?" Nora asked while walking over and standing beside him.

"A bit stiff, but I'm fine." Alex stretched his shoulder.

"That's good. I overheard you telling your friends you're leaving. Is that true?"

"Yeah…Barbra, Josh, and I are heading out in the morning. I wish I could stay, but the captain deemed us useless."

"I'm sorry."

"I never got to thank you for your help back there, Nora. You did a lot for us, thank you."

"It's okay. I didn't mind at all. Besides, I was able to help the great precursors. Not everyone gets to say that." Nora smiled.

"True," Alex chuckled. "Though it's a bit weird, being referred to in the same way as a god."

"Oh, that reminds me, I was wondering if I could ask you a question?"

"Sure, what is it?"

"Do you happen to know who wrote this?" Nora held out the leather book. "I found it years ago during my first dig and have been trying to figure out the author since. The writing is very thought-provoking."

"Let me see," Alex said, grabbing the book and opening the pages.

"I think it might be the journal of some philosopher or something," Nora stated, a thoughtful look crossing her face. "The only problem is, I've never heard mention of their work."

Reading through the entries, Alex smiled as he recognized his own thoughts and handwriting scrawled on each page.

"I don't think you ever will," Alex replied, after handing her back the journal.

"Why not?" Nora asked while flipping through the pages. "Is it just a random book?"

"If it is thought-provoking to you and you enjoy it, does it really matter who wrote it?" Alex smiled before turning to look at the stars.

"I guess you are right."

Epilogue

In the dark, the hum of a thousand watts surged along trails of cold cords and wires. The whirring of computer fans and processors shook off centuries of dust and grime and began their erratic spinning frenzy once more. A single large monitor flickered to life, defying the age of its parts, the diodes inside yellow with age and cracked.

Shapes shifted in the shadows around the weak light of the screen, flowing like loose scraps of fabric in the wind. This was their god, their purpose, so long as they keep rebuilding the forgotten machine, striving toward this singular goal. The time had come to reap the fruits of their labor.

The screen released a momentary burst of sound as an eye digitized and pixilated over the screen. The beings cheered in weird chirps and buzzes, sounding like a flock of birds amidst a beehive. Then suddenly, they all went quiet as their next directive soon became clear. Hastily, they rushed from the shadowy room toward their new goal.

In the dark, a singular eye contemplated its next move.

Ten percent of Wandering Minds Publishing's profit from all book sales is donated to a cause or organization of the author's choice. All sales of this book will contribute toward the Adams State University Theatre Department in Alamosa, Colorado.

* 9 7 8 1 9 5 9 6 6 5 0 2 1 *